A Tale from Horn Harbor

JACK GALBRAITH

PAGE PUBLISHING, INC.
New York, NY

First originally published by Page Publishing, Inc. 2018

ISBN 978-1-64214-108-5 (Paperback)
ISBN 978-1-64214-109-2 (Digital)

Printed in the United States of America

Chapter 1

Hoops was nervous.

He had good reason to be. The red-tailed sea hawk circling above his fishing boat was as big, if not bigger, than Hoops himself.

"Sea hawks are unpredictable," Hoops muttered to Havoc, who was resting on his haunches on the other side of the long wooden tiller. "They can attack you for no reason at all." The shaggy red wolf glanced skyward at the hawk and then promptly returned his sleepy gaze back to the south side of Horn Harbor, toward home.

Hoops glanced over his shoulder at the charcoal gray storm clouds surging in from the sea. The temperature was dropping.

So was the sun.

So was the giant bird of prey.

The hawk's effortless circles had become tighter and tighter as it closed in on the little boat. Hoops instinctively laid his right hand on the short-handled hunter's ax tucked into his broad leather belt beneath a frayed woolen cloak. His left hand remained on the tiller.

"That bird is going to attack us just for the sport of it," he warned Havoc. "Get ready to hit the deck!" With a screech, the hawk dived, wings folded back, talons extended. Hoops dove, too, head-first into a pile of slimy fish on the open deck. He never drew the ax. He covered his head with both hands. There was a loud swish above him, followed by a throaty growl from Havoc and the thump of something falling on the forward deck near the mast.

Then silence.

Cautiously, Hoops raised his head. The hawk had almost disappeared, soaring westward up Horn Harbor. Hoops was wedged between a dogfish, still squirming, and a tuna. Havoc brushed past him, sniffed among the fish for a few seconds, and returned to Hoops with a cylinder-shaped, deerskin-wrapped package between his fangs. Hoops, still on his belly, reached up and retrieved it from the wolf.

"I know what this is," Hoops said in disgust, as he scrambled to his knees and began fumbling with still shaky fingers at the thong that bound the parcel. "I bet it's an invitation from the magus himself. Politely delivered by some vicious creature, as is his custom. And probably just as politely penned." Hoops was right. Rolled up inside the deerskin was a dirty scrap of yellow parchment with the words boldly printed in Wiffinvolk: *Come at once.* Not even a *please* or a signature.

"I don't care if they call my grandfather the Wise One of Horn Harbor. I'm beginning to believe he's finally lost his senses. That hawk might have decided to rip off a hunk of my scalp, just for the fun of it. Why can't the old sorcerer use carrier pigeons like everyone else?"

Hoops brought his boat about and with shortened sail, eased her into a cove flanked by cypress trees and a heavy undergrowth of bayberry bushes. Hoops raised the centerboard and dropped the sail, as they nudged a narrow beach. Havoc leaped ashore first, the bow line between his teeth. He made for a massive cypress stump, did two turns around it with the line, and then squatted, impatiently waiting for Hoops to come ashore and finish securing the vessel. Havoc couldn't tie knots.

Havoc didn't have to wait long. Normally, before leaving the boat, Hoops would first scoop up his catch with a wooden shovel, sort the various fish, and load them into baskets woven from cordgrass. But now, the storm blew in and a wall of wind-driven icy rain slammed into the cove with such ferocity that Hoops couldn't see two paces ahead of himself. He jumped off the bow, secured the line with several half hitches, and despite some pain from an old injury to his right knee, he and Havoc dashed up a barely perceptible trail through the underbrush to the shelter of Hoops's home.

Hoops lived in a tree. Except for a few cave dwellers like his wizard grandfather, Armarugh, or the great Wiffin artist, Humo, Wiffinvolk lived in trees. But Hoops's tree house was different from those of his neighbors.

They had built their elaborate homes on platforms nestled among the spreading branches of mammoth oaks and chestnuts. Hoops's abode was inside a tree—a simple, two-room affair in the trunk of an ancient live oak. You don't enter straight into the tree. You enter through a concealed doorway some distance away and follow a narrow tunnel that leads to the base of the trunk. Then you climb roughly-hewed stairs that spiral their way to the chambers about halfway up the trunk.

During the day, sunlight filtered into Hoop's tiny rooms from former squirrel holes and raccoon hollows. On a clear night, moonbeams bathed the sparsely furnished rooms with a soft glow. Another hole farther up where branches spread out allows fireplace smoke to escape. The gigantic tree had suffered from heart rot, but Hoops had carefully chiseled out all the diseased wood to create his dwelling, leaving the tree healthy and still growing. As small as his home was, Hoops was proud of it. His only serious complaint was the raccoons and squirrels that constantly tried to move back in with him. That was one reason why Hoops tolerated Zaggie, the cat.

"I presume you have received Armarugh's invitation?" It was Zaggie.

The room was engulfed in shadows, disturbed only by flickers of dying firelight in a comer hearth. Hoops could barely make out the cat curled up on a stuffed leather cushion near the stone fireplace.

"It wasn't an invitation. It was a summons," grumbled Hoops.

"I presume you will be leaving to see the Wise One immediately. I read a sense of urgency in his telepathic communication with me," Zaggie said.

"I don't take orders from my grandfather or from a cat, Zaggie," Hoops snapped. "Don't badger me tonight. I'm tired, my knee hurts, and I've got a boatload of fish to gut, scale, split, and salt down. As soon as this storm lets up, that's exactly what I intend to do."

There was a moment of silence. Havoc had gulped down a slab of cured boar meat and was already asleep in a corner. He began to snore.

"As you wish," Zaggie purred. "Please remember that it is not I who give orders. I only serve as a link between the thoughts of your grandfather and you." She paused. "Any shark this evening? You know it's my favorite meal."

"One dogfish."

"I suppose that's better than no shark at all. By the way, you reek of fish. Both you and that silly wolf."

"Don't cats normally like the smell of fish?" Hoops asked.

"But I'm not a normal cat," said Zaggie, as she folded her bat-like wings over her head to take a catnap.

Hoops added wood to the fire. He filled a copper kettle with water and dropped in a fistful of ground sassafras root. Pulling his slimy cloak closely about him, he sat on a fur rug by the fire, massaging his right knee and waiting for his tea to brew and the storm to abate.

Close to the midnight hour, the storm slid off to the north of Horn Harbor, and Hoops was able to tackle his day's catch. For several hours, he worked on the beach by the light of a driftwood fire. An hour before dawn, Hoops wearily mounted the stairs again to his chambers. He had just shed his cloak and was lighting one of his whale oil lamps when Zaggie broke the silence. "The Wise One once again has communicated with me. He has inquired why you delay in seeing him."

"And what did you tell him, Zaggie?"

"I tried to explain to him that his grandson must earn a livelihood, no matter how menial and degrading that livelihood is for a Wiffin, but he declined to hear me through. Armarugh insists that his invitation concerns a matter of great urgency. It was a cloudy communication, perhaps because of the tempest, but I am most positive I detected a spot of blood on his forehead—his way of communicating a warning of impending doom.

"His final words to me," added the winged cat. "And I quote him precisely were: 'Inform Hoops that, for the first time in his

wretched life, he must demonstrate responsibility and dare do something vitally important. I swear by the power and the lesser deities,
this is a matter of life or death for all Wiffinvolk. Indeed, for all Horn
Harbor.'"

Chapter 2

A diffused glow of pale red on the horizon heralded dawn as Hoops and Havoc reached Shadow Cove which Armarugh called home. They beached their craft between two towering dead oak whose gnarled branches grope like skeletal hands trying to snare any passerby. The pair followed a flickering light that bounced along two hands high above a path that wound its way through the marsh grass and oozing black tidal mud to the entrance of the sorcerer's cavern. Just inside the doorway, they were greeted by a venomous hiss from Dodo. Havoc, tail between his legs, hung back behind Hoops.
"She's not going to harm you, Havoc," Hoops whispered. But he, too, stood deathly still.

A guttural voice boomed from deep within the cave. "Allow them entrance, Dodo. It is only my grandson and, I presume, that silly, timid wolf of his."

Hoops and a trembling Havoc moved cautiously along a narrow, dank passageway. Hoops heard Dodo's sharp claws on the flagstone floor as the scaly creature scurried aside to let them pass. They entered a spacious chamber lighted by candles scattered about and a fire in a pit in the middle of the room. Shelves overflowing with ancient manuscripts, scrolls, beakers, bottles of various acidic-smelling liquids, and powders lined the walls—all the paraphernalia of the professional alchemist.

Armarugh, shrouded in his black, hooded cloak, stood by the fire, pouring an amber liquid from a tarnished copper jug into two scratched and dented pewter mugs. He took some dried leaves from a nearby clay pot, crumpled them between his bony fingers, and dropped some into each mug. Then he grasped a red-hot iron poker from the fire, thrust it into the mugs until the liquid bubbled and handed one mug to Hoops. Hoops noticed that the poker's iron handle had scorched Armarugh's hand, and a momentary whiff of burned flesh drifted through the room. But Armarugh showed no sign of pain.

"Theatrics to impress me," Hoops said to himself, as he took the mug and sipped what tasted like hard apple cider laced with aromatic herbs.

Armarugh said, "That will help warm you up and rid you of discomfort in your knee. I notice you're limping again. It's a pity our great surgeon, Zurko, had not yet perfected his skills when you were a wee child and that bear attacked you. Zurko believes it's too late now to repair the damage. Does it bother you often, Hoops?"

Hoops was surprised. Armarugh rarely inquired about his health. "The soreness comes and goes," Hoops replied. "I notice it more in damp, cold weather."

"Then, by all means, please sit over there, closer to the fire," said the wizard, pointing to a pile of fur-covered cushions just inside the ring of crimson light from the fire pit.

Covering his surprise that his grandfather used the word *please*, Hoops sat cross-legged, pulling his damp cloak about him. The old sorcerer took a seat on a wooden bench in a shadowy corner. Armarugh clutched his ebony staff topped by a silver dragon's head in his right hand. In the erratic light, the old man's narrow face appeared to be chiseled from unpolished granite. The wizard always looked tired, but he seemed wearier and worried than usual. Havoc slunk into a dark opposite corner to go to sleep. "You and your wolf companion both reek of fish," Armarugh said. "It is a pity that you, the son of a great Wiffin explorer and cartographer, should have to hunt and fish for a living simply because you declined to immerse yourself in your studies."

"I didn't come here for another lecture, Grandfather," Hoops said testily. The room seemed warmer now, perhaps because of the hot cider he was nursing. He felt a little light-headed, probably from hunger. He hadn't eaten for hours. "Zaggie tells me this was a matter of great importance or something like that."

"Indeed, Hoops. Most important and most urgent. But first, I must remind you of a little history. A study you always belittled as a worthless rehash of a past that cannot be changed."

"I'm listening." Hoops stifled a yawn.

"Indeed, as even you must know, there are two city-states on opposite shores of Dark Harbor, Sar, and Lugh. They have been at war with each other for eons. Neither can achieve total victory. Both city-states are too powerful, too well fortified to be conquered. Just recently, Queen Saragata of Sar led yet another massive attack against Lugh. As usual, the outcome was indecisive, although, as customary, both sides claimed victory."

"So?" Hoops interrupted. "Let the Sariens and Lughs kill each other. That's their affair, not a concern for Wiffinvolk."

"Indeed, their war is their affair. But have you not wondered, my dear grandson, why both the Sariens and Lughs have left us alone for generations? We engage in a form of commerce with them, it's true. They pay us dearly for services that only talented Wiffinvolk can render them. For example, last month, our famed goldsmith and jewelry designer, Haro, was commissioned by Queen Saragata to design special jewelry for herself and her court's ladies to wear at the festival honoring their God of War, Brutius. That arrangement alone put a substantial sum, not only in Haro's pocket, but in the coffers of our Assembly of Elders for public use."

Hoops, whose empty stomach was growling, spied a wooden trough with a chunk of crusty sourdough bread on the stone floor close by the fire. Without asking Armarugh's permission, he walked over to it and pried off a hunk, resumed his seat, and said before beginning to gnaw, "So? That's trade. After all, even my Wiffinvolk neighbors pay me for salted fish and cured game, the fruits of my few talents, limited as those talents might be by your lofty standards."

The Wise One shifted his dragon staff from one hand to another. He exhaled sharply. "You never cease to disappoint me, Hoops. Has the question never entered your brain as to why the Sariens or Lughs don't send one of their war fleets to Horn Harbor and enslave the entire Wiffinvolk population? Wouldn't it be much cheaper for them to have Wiffin slaves solve their engineering problems, design their jewelry, or whatever? Under a Sarien whip, our beloved Haro would design only the best jewelry for Queen Saragata and at no cost to her at all."

Hoops chewed on another morsel of bread and studied his slimy sea boots. "Then please enlighten me. Why haven't they made a move on Horn Harbor?"

"They are afraid to."

"That is ridiculous! The Sariens or the Lughs afraid of us? They are all warriors, especially the Lughs. Both the Lughs and the Sariens are bigger than we, Wiffinvolk. They have the finest weapons. We don't have any weapons at all, except perhaps a few sporting bows. They have war fleets. We don't have any ships because being a sea-man is beneath a Wiffin's dignity. We have a Defense Council, but it's been leaderless for generations. In fact, I've never heard of it actually having a meeting. It's said that, in ancient times, we, Wiffinvolk, were famous for being brave heroes, but I bet you couldn't find a single Wiffin now who would know what to do with a sword if you handed it to him. In short, dear Grandfather, your statement that the Sariens or the Lughs are afraid is utter nonsense."

Armarugh rose from his bench and glided over to one of the shelves piled with rolls of parchment. They looked like navigational charts to Hoops. The sorcerer began rummaging among them. His back was to Hoops, but he continued to speak.

"What you say is true, Hoops. Still, trust me. They are afraid and for two reasons. The first, the lesser one, is that neither city-state wants to divert from their defenses a large portion of their forces for an attack on us. The second reason and the most important, is their fear of the powerful sorceress, Tajine. She has a certain talisman of awesome power. Whoever possesses the talisman can devastate a city-state with a simple invocation. And for many generations, Tajine has sworn she will use this talisman against either Sar or Lugh if either of them threatens Horn Harbor."

"Doesn't she live in a desolate region in the north of Sar territory? Isn't she Sarien?" Hoops asked. "Why would she care the slightest about our fate?"

Armarugh faced Hoops with a rolled parchment in hand. "Because her mother was a Wiffin, Tajine has deep-seated loyalties to our homeland." Hoops started to say something, but the Wise One cut him off with a loud tap of his staff. "I anticipate your next query, Hoops. Why, you ask, do I now say we, Wiffinvolk, are suddenly in any danger?"

"The thought had occurred to me," replied Hoops. "So, please explain."

Armarugh said nothing for a few moments. The shrouded form moved out of the shadows over to a long wooden table strewn with more jars, bottles, stone mortars, and the inevitable manuscripts. He swept his hand across the center of the table, shoving the clutter aside to clear a space for the chart which he then unrolled carefully. He dragged a lighted stubby candle over to the edge of the document and ordered Hoops to approach.

"This is a chart of Dark Harbor showing the Sarien coastline. It was one of the last maps done by your famous father before he and your mother were lost at sea on an expedition a year later. It is a beautiful and very accurate work. Had you ever studied geography, you would have been very familiar with it." There was a soft tone of reverence in Armarugh's voice. The softness didn't last long. "But you elected not to study geography, so you've never seen this masterpiece."

"So I haven't seen it! So what?" Hoops was getting angry. "You haven't answered my question. Why all the sudden urgency with this talisman thing?"

"Because Tajine is dying. The moment she's dead, the Sariens and the Lughs will battle each other to seize control of Tajine's castle and the talisman she has hidden there. Trust me, Hoops, the winner of that fight will leave no stone unturned to find the talisman. Remember, the city-state that controls the talisman can devastate the other and then turn its undivided attention to enslaving us and the rest of the known world."

"Why is Tajine dying? I've always heard the great sorceress would live forever. She's practically immortal, like a goddess."

"Alas, she ventured one experiment too many in the realm of lycanthropy, and it's proving fatal."

"Isn't that something to do with werewolves?" Hoops instinctively threw a glance at Havoc. The wolf was snoring gently.

"Not always. The word denotes the magical transformation into a beast, any beast. I warned her about this dangerous activity, but she was too confident in her own powers to heed my advice. She now informs me she does not expect to last much beyond this lunar month of Tor."

"By Zob! That's not much time," Hoops exclaimed.

Hoops got a glance of reproach from his grandfather. "No need to take a deity's name in vain, Hoops, no matter how minor the deity."

"Sorry, Grandfather," Hoops muttered. Then quickly added, "Why tell me all this? You should be warning the Assembly of Elders, not that they can do much about it."

Armarugh inched the candle closer to the chart. He hunched over the table and appeared to be studying it closely. There was a long silence.

"Well?" said Hoops.

"I have informed a select number of them. They agree with my plan," said the wizard.

"What plan?" asked Hoops.

"We must go to Tajine's Dourghoul Keep, spirit the talisman away and bring it back safely to Horn Harbor before she dies and the Sariens and Lugh learn of her demise."

"That's absurd. It's suicidal. You'd need a powerful army to tramp across Sarien territory uninvited. I told you, Grandfather, we don't have any army. We don't even have ships to get to Dark Harbor."

"But we have you, my dear grandson."

The chamber turned to ice. Hoops felt tightness in his chest as if a giant python had coiled itself around him and was squeezing the life out of his body. He felt dizzy. He tried to speak, but at first, his throat was restricted. Finally, he found his voice.

"In the name of Zob, what do you expect me to do, Grandfather?"

"Sail to Sar and secretly bring back the talisman for safekeeping."

"I can't believe you're my grandfather! You're asking me, your grandson, to commit suicide. You know the moment the Sariens find out what I'm up to, they'll slap me into a dungeon or even kill me outright!"

Armarugh shook his head. "You don't listen to me, Hoops. I used the word *secretly*. You are an accomplished seaman, the only one we have in Wiffinvolk. You alone possess the skills of a professional hunter and trapper—qualities needed to find a way through the wilds of northern Sar where Tajine lives, and return with the talisman undetected and unscathed. You, alone, among us Wiffins have the talent to carry out this crucial mission."

"Talent?" Hoops shouted. "You've always told me I have no talent."

"Perhaps, I was mistaken," replied the grim-faced wizard. "I have always judged you solely by Wiffin standards. But we face a new challenge, Hoops, and new values must be established. Both in my perception of you and your perception of yourself."

Amarugh paused to offer Hoops another cup of spiced cider. Hoops felt a little light-headed, a shade giddy. He sniffed the dregs of cider in his mug. The aroma of crushed anise seeds mixed with something he couldn't identify seemed overpowering. He adamantly rejected a second cup.

"I'm alive now, Grandfather. But if I accept your mission, I may not be much longer."

"Indeed, you're alive. But is that all there is to life, just existing? Surely there must be a purpose to life?" The wizard's eyes were glowing embers embedded in ice. "Now, finally, you have a purpose for living, Hoops. You have a responsibility to your homeland. Are you too cowardly to accept that responsibility?"

"I'm not a coward!" Hoops flared.

"Then prove it!" shouted his grandfather.

Hoops leapt to his feet and flung the empty pewter mug across the room. It crashed against a stone wall and clattered to the floor.

"By Zob, I will prove it," he shouted back.

Chapter 3

For three days, they sailed south following the coast but staying well out to sea, out of sight of the mainland. The stiff onshore wind from the east had been steady and Hoops kept the vessel on a broad reach, making better time than he had expected to leeward the ragged, towering cliffs of Desolate Isle sprouted from the cerulean blue sea like threatening giants. They were now in Sarien waters, rumored to be teeming with pirates and warships. Well off the port beam, a thin line of angry gray clouds marred the cold, pristine sky.

"Looks like heavy weather coming," Hoops said to Zaggie, who had just left her usual perch on the bowsprit to curl up for a nap in the cockpit where Hoops sat at the tiller. Havoc was out of sight, sleeping in a squat deckhouse that Hoops had hastily constructed before they departed Horn Harbor.

Streams of green seaweed drifted lazily in the current. For two days, a horned, green-eyed sea serpent, twice as long as the boat, had been playing in their wake. Zaggie assured Hoops the serpent was simply curious and meant them no harm. But Hoops kept a close, suspicious eye on the creature.

"Why did the Wise One order me to bring along a critter like you on a suicidal mission like this?" Hoops asked the winged cat. "I'm surprised you agreed to do something this stupid."

"You agreed to accept this mission. I'm surprised at you."

"False pride," Hoops muttered. "Armarugh accused me of being a coward if I didn't accept. Besides, I think he gave me some kind of drug to make me more receptive to his arguments. I was in a sort of a daze after I quaffed down that spiced cider."

Hoops forgot that Zaggie had neglected to answer his question. His thoughts drifted back to the fateful morning in Armarugh's cavern. Besides labeling Hoops a coward, his grandfather had played upon the remnants of Hoops's pride in himself. Hoops was astonished that his arch critic recognized his talents as a sailor and woodsman. Hoops had fallen for the flattery, and now he cursed himself for it.

Hoops was yanked out of his reverie by a squeal from Zaggie. "Watch out for the sea serpent!"

Hoops jerked his head around in time to see the leviathan slicing through the water inches below the surface. It passed directly beneath the boat's transom. The boat shook violently. The tiller ripped from Hoops's grasp and clattered to the deck. There came a sound of wood splintering. The boat swung into the wind and stopped dead in the water.

The craft's wooden rudder surfaced and bobbed in the waves several yards to the stem. "By Zob! Look what your friendly sea serpent has done, Zaggie. He's ripped off our rudder, probably with a tail fluke when he passed under us." Hoops immediately shed his cloak and yanked off his sea boots, preparing to dive overboard to retrieve the floating rudder.

"He is a she, Hoops," Zaggie corrected him. "And she didn't mean to cause the accident. She was just being playful."

Before Hoops was able to draw up enough nerve to plunge into the icy sea, the serpent had circled around and, with her long snoot, began gently nudging the rudder back to the boat. A few moments later, Hoops was able to snag it with a boat hook and drag it aboard. The sea serpent retreated a short distance, flicked its scaly tail twice as a goodbye gesture, and dove out of sight.

"Goodbye," said Zaggie.

"Good riddance," muttered Hoops.

Hoops quickly examined the damaged equipment. "Great! The pintles were ripped right out. We are going to have to make shore and beach the boat so I can work up under the stern to do some repairs."

"Pintles?"

"Yes, Zaggie. For your information, those are the fastenings on the leading edge of the rudder. They fit into other fastenings called gudeons to hold the rudder to the boat." He paused and added, "I'll make a seaman or seacat out of you yet, Zaggie."

"Well, to add more brightness to our day" said Zaggie. "That storm seems to be gaining on us. And I see three ships with black sails some distance out to sea. Pirates, I imagine."

"You do make my day, Zaggie!" With that, Hoops swiftly rigged a makeshift rudder using a sturdy oar lashed to the broken-off tiller. "I don't believe we have much choice but to seek refuge on Desolate Isle. According to my father's map, that mass of sheer rock is surrounded by a reef with just a few channels through it. There should be a safe cove somewhere inside that reef, hopefully with a sandy beach or two. Let's hope we can get there before the storm or the pirates catch us in the open."

Hoops ordered Zaggie to keep a sharp eye on the three vessels while he brought his craft about, easing the mainsheet until the boom swung well out over the side to take full advantage of the breeze. Hoops scanned the reef of surf-pounded rocks ahead, searching for signs of a channel. At last, he spotted a gap in the line of foamy white and adjusted course.

"That channel doesn't look very wide, and I can only pray to the powers that it's deep enough," Hoops said. "How are our companions doing?"

"The ships are holding a course northward. I do not believe they have spotted us. At least, not yet," replied Zaggie. Havoc, wakened by the collision with the sea serpent, stood beside Hoops, his muzzle jutting over the gunwale, watching the ships on the horizon.

A short distance from the channel's entrance, Hoops realized just how narrow it was and how fast the incoming tide surged through it. He also noticed for the first time that each side of the entrance was graced with a weathered stake. Each stake had a bleached skull nailed to it. The skulls were adorned with horns.

"Trollard skulls," Zaggie informed Hoops. "They're like goats but can be very nasty when threatened."

The wind veered to the north, and Hoops had to haul in the mainsheet rapidly to keep the little boat on course. The roar of the swells breaking on the rocks on either side was deafening as they plunged into the channel entrance. The boat careened and bounced off one side of the channel to another. Spume-speckled black boulders closed in on them. Hoops involuntarily shut his eyes and tensed in anticipation of a jarring crash and the fatal sound of planking being ripped apart beneath his feet.

Suddenly, silence. He opened his eyes and saw only the placid water of a cove around him. "By Zob, we've made it!" he shouted.

"I did not for a moment anticipate we would not," said Zaggie calmly. "I have complete faith in your seamanship, my dear Hoops."

The boat drifted in with the tide to a narrow shingle of hard, packed sand at the base of a towering cliff.

Although Zaggie could have spread her wings and flown across the strip of ankle-deep water that separated the boat's bow from the dry beach, she insisted Hoops carry her. "Cats don't like even taking a chance of getting wet," she told him.

"I thought you told me you weren't an ordinary cat," Hoops growled back at her but, as always, he caved in to her demands.

When all three voyagers finally reached the beach, Hoops secured the boat and immediately scanned the shoreline for pieces of driftwood which could be used to repair the steering mechanism. Nothing.

Meanwhile, Havoc trotted down the beach, relieved himself against the base of the cliff and sniffed at something near the water's edge. Hoops and Zaggie followed.

A shiny object glittered in the sand. Hoops picked up a small, bright piece of red coral encased in a circle of gold.

"An earring," observed Zaggie. "Crudely made. Certainly not by any Wiffinvolk craftsman. Strange that it should be lying here."

"It must have washed ashore from some shipwreck," said Hoops. He placed the ornament in the small leather pouch hanging from his belt. "Let's declare it a souvenir of Desolate Isle." He glanced around at the high cliffs above. "According to my father's account, Desolate Isle was uninhabited."

"Then I doubt there are any Sariens about. I am certain there is little on this chunk of rock to plunder, and Sariens do not waste their time on other activities," Zaggie volunteered.

"Perhaps you speak too harshly of the Sariens," Hoops said. "After all, they have done no harm to Wiffinvolk for many generations. And they pay well for our services and learned advice."

"Only because they have no other choice at the moment," replied the winged cat. "Trust me. Don't trust them. I know them better than you do, even better than the Wise One."

"Oh. Why is that, Zaggie?"

"You will learn why in due time," she answered. "Meanwhile, I will find a perch on a ledge somewhere up that cliff and keep a watch for any sign of a ship cruising nearby. I suggest you lower our ship's mast. It might be visible to a passing vessel with a sharp lookout in the crow's nest."

Hoops agreed. He returned to his boat, quickly loosened the shrouds and fore and back stays and unstepped the mast, laying it on the deck to one side of the flimsy deckhouse. "Now Havoc and I are off to find wood somewhere on this forsaken island," he told Zaggie. "I don't relish having to tear up perfectly good deck planks to do the necessary repairs if I don't absolutely have to." He glanced at the cliffs, shook his head, then looked up the cove toward the entrance to a ravine which might snake its way to a plateau. "There must be trees up there, even if they are twisted and dwarfed by the constant wind blasting this island," he announced. Then to Havoc, "Let's get moving quickly. Evening is fast upon us, and I don't like the idea of negotiating this land in the dark."

The sun was a crimson ball sinking rapidly into a frenzy of roiling black storm clouds when the pair abandoned their efforts and elected to return to the cove. They had found nothing growing on the high plateau of Desolate Isle, save patches of lichen and an occasion tuft of wind-tossed grass struggling to survive in crevices between outcrops of black rock. It had turned bitterly cold.

Retracing their steps through the ravine back to the boat was rough going. Enormous boulders littered the bottom of the ravine.

In some places, rockslides had practically sealed it off. Then darkness set in.

Twice, Hoops lost his footing and fell sideways, the little ax in his belt clanging loudly against a barely visible boulder. Each time, he felt a sharp pain in his right knee. A third time, he tripped, falling against the rocks.

"Hear that?" came a voice. "Something moving down there." The speaker had a Sarien accent. He was high above them on the lip of the ravine. Hoops could barely make out two silhouettes against the twilight sky.

A second voice spoke. "Maybe it is our quarry. Quick! Light a torch and let's climb down there. We might get the General's reward yet."

Rapid clicks of flint against steel were followed by a flare of orange light. Hoops froze. Havoc growled.

"Hear that sound?" the first voice said in disappointment. "That's not our creature. Sounds more like a wild animal or maybe a trollard. Forget climbing down there. Let's get back to camp before we can't see where we're going."

A grunt of agreement followed, and the voices moved away. Hoops exhaled sharply and turned to find Havoc. The red wolf had disappeared in the darkness. "Probably ran to the boat in pure terror," he muttered to himself and struck out once more toward the cove.

He had gone only a short distance when he thought he caught a faint glimmer of light to his left. He approached the side of the ravine and found himself at the entrance of what appeared to be a cave. The hint of a flame flickered inside. A trollard home? He took another step closer to the entrance. He was about to take one more when something sliced through the air just past his right ear. He heard the unmistakable twang of a bowstring.

"One more step and the next shaft will be right through your worthless neck." The accent was Sarien. The voice was a girl's.

Chapter 4

"I'm not budging," Hoops promised. His voice quivered. Whether from cold or fear or both, he couldn't decide.

"Wise decision," the girl said. Her tone was as icy as the night air outside the cave's entrance.

A burst of flame caused Hoops to involuntarily shut his eyes. When he reopened them, he saw a smoke-shrouded form of a girl standing on the far side of a crackling fire in the center of a narrow, stone-vaulted cavern. She held a short bow nocked with an arrow, aimed, Hoops was convinced, right between his eyes.

"Shed your cloak and stretch out your arms, hands open and palms facing me, so I can see them," the girl demanded.

Hoops did as ordered. Without his cloak, the night wind racing through the ravine stabbed like frozen needles. His whole body began trembling. "I'm freezing out here," he blurted. "Can't I come in and stand by your fire? I mean you no harm."

"Maybe, maybe not" was the reply. "Drop that pathetic little belt ax on the ground. The hunting knife, too." Hoops obeyed. "Now tum around. I can't believe you don't have a real weapon strapped on your back."

Hoops turned around. The temperature was dropping fast. His teeth were chattering. His bad knee throbbed.

The girl said, "No other weapons that I can see, and you don't sound Sarien. Come inside the cave, but stay on your side of the fire until I decide your fate."

Hoops stepped inside. Warmth at last, but immediately, he began gagging. A sharp acid odor permeated the cave, momentarily suffocating him.

"It's trollard dung smoke," the girl said. "I'm afraid we don't have the luxury of abundant firewood around here." Hoops sensed a hint of humor in her voice. "You'll get used to it, if you live so long. Now, sit down, warm yourself, and tell me who you are and what you're doing on Desolate Isle."

"My name is Hoops. I'm a Wiffin and a fisherman by trade," Hoops responded between coughing fits, as he sat down on a flat rock as close to the flames as possible. He began massaging his knee. "We were following a school of green rockfish south when we encountered this stupid sea serpent." He related the incident with the reptile.

"*We?* Who's here with you?"

"A cat and a wolf." His knee was feeling better, but his stomach was growling. He hadn't eaten for hours.

"I thought I saw a panicked animal race by the cave entrance before you came crashing through the ravine like a clumsy bull. The creature was too small for a trollard, although I'm expecting a visit from them tonight," the girl noted. She started to lower her bow, but abruptly took aim at Hoops again.

"You are lying. Wiffins are all artisans or intellectuals. Creatures of that ilk. I've never heard tell of a Wiffin fisherman." Ice returned to her voice. "You could be another bounty hunter General Itus has sent after me. Eight nasty little Yargos came here by boat to search for me a few days ago. They're gone, but a group of regular Sarien legionnaires are now on this island, scouring the hills."

Hoops raised his hands in the air. "I don't know who General Itus is, and I'm not looking for you. Besides, you have to admit, for a bounty hunter or a soldier, I didn't come very well armed. I swear by the powers, I sincerely mean you no harm."

The girl did not respond immediately. She stepped forward a few paces to examine Hoops more closely. The powerful recurve bow remained steady in her hands at full draw. *By Zob,* thought Hoops nervously. *For a girl, she's got tremendous strength.* She was still in the shadows, and although Hoops couldn't see her clearly, she looked rather slender.

"You appear to be harmless enough." She relaxed the bow and moved into the circle of firelight. She was slender. Hoops noticed she was wearing leather leggings with high leather boots like himself. She had a sleeveless fur vest over a dirt stained tunic and carried a long-bladed, bone-handled dagger tucked in a sash around her waist. Her youthful face was narrow with a wide, unsmiling mouth. Her large eyes were polished ebony, intense but humorless. Tangled red hair streamed down over her shoulders. She looked haggard and ill-nourished.

Hoops took advantage of an apparent truce. In the most cheerful tone he could muster, he asked, "And what is your name, young lady?"

"My name is Javala, daughter of the Gretien clan leader, Javalius. And I'm as old as you are, maybe older, Wiffin."

"Do I take it, then, that you are not Sarien?"

"Of course, I'm Sarien. But the kingdom of Sar is made up of a lot of different tribes and clans. I'm surprised that you, a Wiffin, wouldn't know that! I was always led to believe all Wiffins were well-educated." Javala had lowered the bow to her side, but Hoops saw her fingers tighten around the weapon's grip.

"Of course, I know something about the kingdom of Sar. It's just that I've never heard the name Gretien before. That's the truth, I swear to Zob!" he said hastily, hoping to defuse another confrontation.

"Who is Zob?"

"The God of dim-witted Wiffins. Sometimes I think I'm the only one who has to pray to him."

The girl seated herself on a flat rock opposite him. She removed the arrow from the bowstring and laid both instruments in the dirt within easy reach. There was a faint trace of warmth in her eyes.

"Who is the General Itus, and why are these people looking for you?" Hoops asked.

The warmth vanished. "Lord General Itus heads up Queen Saragata's army of legionnaires, the ones who raided our camp without warning and killed most of my clan, including my father and mother. Maybe my young brother, too. There was blood everywhere. I was fortunate to escape the massacre so that someday I will have a chance to kill that grotesque Itus myself."

"Why did they attack you?"

"Hatred. Many years ago, my father dueled with Itus, and as a result, Itus lost one hand. He now wears an iron claw. The general was waiting for an excuse to take revenge. We are nomadic herdsmen and pay our taxes in meat to the kingdom of Sar. A mysterious disease struck our herds this year, and we couldn't pay our taxes on time and still have enough to feed ourselves. Itus, with Queen Saragata's blessing, marched into our land to force us to pay. Itus sent an emissary to our camp to request a meeting with my father the following morning to negotiate a settlement. Of course, my father agreed to the talks. But during the night, the legionnaires took us by surprise, with that treacherous Itus in the front ranks."

While she was talking, Javala's right hand was gripping the dagger at her waist. Her knuckles were white. She was looking straight at Hoops, but he wondered if she was seeing him.

"As I was crawling through brambles to safety on a hillside overlooking our burning tents, I saw the legionnaires slaughtering what livestock still existed. Itus wanted personal revenge, not taxes! I swear by the Great Power that I will kill Itus one day. Mark my words, Wiffin."

"No doubt you will, if given the chance," Hoops mumbled.

"What did you say, Hoops?"

Hoops didn't have a chance to reply. There was rumble of sharp hooves on the rocks outside the cave, and suddenly, a goatlike creature with red eyes and vicious-looking horns loomed in the entrance. The beast bowed its head several times at Javala, then turned to eye Hoops suspiciously.

"Don't be alarmed," the girl told Hoops. "They are trollards, and this big one is the herd leader. I can communicate with them. After all, we Gretiens are herdsmen and know how to deal with grazing animals."

The girl then stood up and approached the animal, patting it on the head between its horns. She reached over and retrieved a partially burned piece of driftwood from the fire. Using it as a torch, she approached one wall of the cave and held the light close to a charcoal drawing of a trollard. It resembled the trollard standing before her. The shaggy animal made a loud grunting noise, echoed by a chorus of similar grunts from the beasts gathered just outside the cave.

"I'm glad you approve," Javala said to the trollard. "Now I want you to do something for me."

Taking a lump of charcoal out of a pocket in her vest, she rapidly drew the outline of a man carrying a spear and shield and wearing what appeared to Hoop to be a plumed helmet. Next, Javala touched the tips of the trollard's horns and then viciously jabbed at the figure on the stone wall with two fingers. The trollard dropped to its front knees for a moment, then straightened back up. There were more grunts from the herd outside. Once more, Javala patted the creature on the head, and the trollard turned and left the cave.

"What was the significance of all that, Javala?"

"The trollards have adopted me, so to speak. And they like to see drawings of themselves."

"What about that other drawing, the soldier?"

Javala smiled. "That is a typical Sarien legionnaire, although I admit, I draw poorly. But I got the message across to the trollard leader."

"What message?"

"For the trollards to kill them," Javala replied. "Or at least drive them back to their boat and off this island. There are a dozen, maybe more, thrashing around this island, and I have few arrows left in my quiver."

"I heard a couple of men talking above the ravine before I stumbled onto your hideout. They said something about a reward."

"I heard them, too, Wiffin. Itus has a reward out for me, dead or alive."

"Why is he so anxious to get you, Javala?"

"Because he is afraid that I, the daughter of Javalius, may someday regroup my scattered clansmen and lead them into battle against the kingdom of Sar. And he's right. I will, and I'll win," she added.

Once again, she fingered the handle of her dagger. Hoops's empty stomach uttered an agonized growl.

"You sound hungry, Hoops," Javala said. She flashed a wide smile. "I hope you don't mind moss hare roasted over trollard dung. It's the best I can offer. Except for the hares, trollards, and an occasional scrawny fox, nothing else lives here. Not even seabirds."

She reached into a leather pouch lying beside her and took out a lump of blackened meat. She sliced off a large piece with her dagger and tossed it to Hoops. "It's cold but you can warm it up over what's left of the fire if you like."

Hoops didn't bother. Despite its strong odor, he bit off a mouthful without hesitation. It tasted as bad as it smelled, but his stomach was dictating the terms.

"How did you get here?" he asked the girl between mouthfuls. "By boat?"

"I know nothing about boats. The only water we have in our land is found in wells or small streams flowing down from the high mountains. I came here by accident. I hastily put together a driftwood raft when I reached the seacoast, just ahead of Itus and his Sariens. I had expected a south wind to push the raft down the coast, out of the Sarien trap. But instead, the raft drifted to this forsaken island. For a time, I thought I would just drift out to sea and die."

"You were caught in the Great Sarien current which flows out to sea, no matter the wind direction. You were lucky to have drifted here," Hoops told her. "If you had missed this island, you would have drifted across the sea and fallen off the edge of the world."

"I had heard that Wiffins think our world is round, like a ball."

"Some Wiffins do, like my wizard grandfather. I don't." The fire was dying, and the cave drew colder.

"Do I have your permission to retrieve my cloak which I dropped on the ground just outside? I hope it's still in one piece after that herd of trollards trampled on it."

Javala nodded.

Hoops found his cloak intact and returned to the fire. He decided to leave his belt ax and hunting knife outside on the ground. He had no intention of telling Javala about the small skinning knife out of sight in his sea boot. He didn't want to alarm the Gretien girl and start her fidgeting again with her bow. Javala sat silently, chin resting in her hands, while Hoops finished his meal.

"You said you have a boat, didn't you? You could take me back to the mainland so that I might go in search of my clansmen," she said suddenly.

"But I need to repair the rudder before I can continue any voyage, especially one of several leagues from here to the mainland, fighting the Great Sarien current all the way."

"What is a rudder?"

Hoops explained it was a steering device. "There is another boat here, the one that the Yargo bounty hunters came in. You could use that. I would try to use it, but it is a big boat and I know nothing about boats or the sea. I'd probably end up drifting over the edge of the world."

Hoops asked Javala to describe it. She did her best, using phrases like *a big stick in the middle,* referring to the mast. When she was done, it was evident to Hoops that the craft was a typical poorly designed Sarien war vessel. It would be too big, draw too much water, and rely on a number of oarsmen rather than sail to get anywhere. Not at all suited for Hoops's mission. But it would have a rudder he might be able to adapt to his smaller, shallow draft vessel.

"Will you show me where it is, Javala?"

"I will, provided you promise to take me back to the mainland."

"I promise, provided I can make the rudder fit my boat," Hoops said. "Then, I shall take you to the boat at dawn. It's not far from here, but we had best be very careful. There may be a score of Sarien legionnaires about, unless the trollards get them first. Meanwhile, I suggest we both get a good night's sleep." Javala pulled her furry vest close about her and curled up on the cave floor, head resting on a flat rock. Hoops pulled his cloak about him and stretched out as comfortably as he could by the smoldering fire.

"Javala?"

"Yes, Hoops."

"Where are the Yargos, the ones who came in that boat? You said they're gone, but how did they leave without their vessel?"

"Trust me, Hoops, they're gone. Their bodies are in the sea."

"Did the trollards kill them?" Hoops inquired.

"No. Now please try to get a good night's rest, Wiffin. It is late." Javala yawned.

"Who did kill them, Javala?"

"I did." She yawned once more and went to sleep.

Chapter 5

"It's time to get moving, Hoops."

Hoops opened his eyes to see Javala standing over him. Daylight struggled through the lingering smoke in the cave. Javala had her bow and quiver slung over her shoulders, and she held Hoops's ax and knife in her hands. He jumped to his feet and immediately grimaced in pain from cramps and soreness—the results of a very uncomfortable night on the gravelly cave floor.

Javala held out his ax and knife. "I trust you will need these tools to work on your boat. Let's pray it doesn't take long. I hope to be on the mainland before nightfall." She turned and strolled out into the sunlit ravine. Hoops dragged his aching body after her.

She led the way to a narrow path that brought them out of the ravine onto the barren plateau high above the dark green sea. The sky was clear, and the weather unexpectedly warm. Hoops folded up his cloak and tossed it over his shoulder. He gazed westward over the water. The mainland was out of sight. He spotted a red sail on the horizon.

"That is a Sarien craft," he told Javala. "Let's hope it is not coming here."

"It's not. Those are the Sarien legionnaires making haste home. While you were sleeping in this morning, the leader of the trollard herd met me. I gathered from his grunts and gestures that the herd surrounded the encamped soldiers at dawn, and the Sariens opted to flee without a fight. The trollard leader was very pleased with himself. However, the creature is saddened that I'm leaving the island."

They trudged along the edge of the cliffs. At length, they spotted a narrow, deep water cove below them. The Yargos' boat was riding at anchor. It was as Hoops envisioned, a poorly designed craft listing to port, probably from a leaking seam on that side of the vessel. But it had a rudder.

Hoops, with eager assistance from Javala, was able to remove the rudder and get it ashore. They had to swim out to the ship and back to manage this, and Hoops imagined this was Javala's first bath in many days. He was hopeful that it would rid Javala of the dung smoke odor that lingered around her despite a fresh sea breeze sweeping over them.

It took them several hours to transport the heavy, oversized rudder up the cliffs, across the plateau, and back down to Hoops's boat on the other side of the island. They were greeted by an ashamed Havoc, who tried to ingratiate himself with his master by licking his boots, and a surly Zaggie who glowered at Javala and refused to talk to her.

"That girl is nothing but trouble," Zaggie told Hoops when she had him alone, while Javala and Havoc played a game of fetch the stick. "Trust me, Hoops. I just know she will jeopardize our mission if she accompanies us anywhere."

"I've promised her I'll ferry her over to the mainland and let her go ashore south of the Black River. I told her I'll then sail north, back up the coast looking for green rockfish. We will sail north but we will land near the mouth of the river, quite a distance away. We'll then hide our boat in the marshes there and continue our mission on foot. I hope, Zaggie, you're up to a lot of walking?"

Zaggie shook her head. "My instincts tell me this is a big, mistake and I always trust my feline instincts."

"Trust my instincts this time, Zaggie," Hoops told the cat. "Please, at least, try to be civil to the girl until we put her ashore. She's been through a lot."

But Zaggie refused to be civil despite Javala's repeated efforts to stroke the cat or engage her in conversation. Meanwhile, Hoops, with the aid of his tool chest and assistance from Javala, succeeded in reshaping the bulky Sarien rudder to fit his boat. Once mounted to the transom with the long steering tiller attached, he and Javala stepped the sturdy mast in an upright position, securing it with several long, supporting lines or *stays* and *shrouds*, as Hoops called them.

They took a break while Hoops gave Javala a simplified lecture on the basics of sailing. She listened attentively and asked numerous questions, especially about the many nautical terms Hoops used.

"Sailing sounds like a lot of fun," she commented, as the two munched on stale bread and fresh clams Havoc had pawed up from the sand along the water line.

"It can be, provided there are no severe storms or the wind doesn't die and you're becalmed, or you don't have a collision with a hyperactive sea serpent. If this breeze holds steady the rest of the afternoon, we should make landfall well before dark," Hoops said. "I suggest we hoist sail now and take maximum advantage of the weather. Remember, we'll be bucking the very current that brought you here."

The tide was outgoing and the sea tranquil. Hoops was able to maneuver his boat without mishap through the narrow channel in the reef past the flanking posts adorned with bleached trollard skulls. He asked Javala if she knew who might have put them there, but she just shook her head.

Once at sea, Hoops shouted "Coming about," and put the tiller hard over to swing the boat on a new course. Despite his earlier safety lecture to Javala, she forgot to duck her head until the last second and almost was knocked overboard by the craft's sail-bearing boom as it swept across the deck to adjust to the change in the wind direction.

"Sorry about that," she said sheepishly.

The first hour, Javala's face had a greenish tinge about it, and Hoops knew she was fighting off seasickness despite calm water and the gentle motion of the boat. He refused her request to lie down inside the little cabin. "Stay out in the fresh air and keep your eyes on the horizon. That will help." It did. Once she felt better, she launched into an enthusiastic round of questions about the boat and everything on it, even the purpose of the few hooks Hoops had aboard to fish for supper during their voyage.

After he had exhausted her seemingly endless stream of questions, Hoops asked her, "What are your plans after I drop you off on the mainland?"

"I will cross the coastal plain, go around the southern base of Gauntlet Mountain, and then head into the highlands in search of what remains of my clan. Hopefully, they have taken refuge in the lands of the Skaggs. I am also hopeful there will be enough warriors alive that we can reorganize and begin ambushing Sarien patrols invading our grazing lands, or maybe even start attacking Sarien outposts to the south."

Hoops was silent for a moment. "I don't want to appear pessimistic, Javala, but it sounds like your plans depend too much on just hoping. Besides, General Itus sounds like a persistent fellow, and probably he's scouring the countryside for you right now."

"I am sure he is," the girl replied. "But I have evaded his legionnaires before, and I'll do so again. If I make it to Skagg territory, I'll be safe. The Skaggs may be tiny, furry creatures, but they are deadly with their blowguns and poison darts and they hate all humans, especially Sarien soldiers. Even the bravest legionnaires are fearful of Skaggs."

"But you said you'd be safe with them?"

"We, Gretiens, are accepted by the Skaggs. My father saved the life of the Skagg chief, Yukman, years ago and ever since, the little creatures have befriended us. As a child, I used to play with Yukman's offspring. When Skaggs are very young, they're actually cute." She smiled.

While Hoops and Javala were talking, a sulking Zaggie was curled up at the foot of the mast, pretending to be asleep. But Hoops knew, from the twitching of the cat's ears, she was listening to every word.

Havoc, meanwhile, was snoring contently, his head in Javala's lap. "You should get some sleep, too," Hoops told the girl. Javala rolled up her fur vest to make a pillow and promptly fell asleep on the deck while Hoops manned the tiller. The following wind was holding steady, and he was making better time than anticipated. He was fast approaching a wide sandy beach. Behind the beach were high sand dunes plumed with sea oats waving in unison in the breeze. In the distance loomed a mass of black granite, Gauntlet Mountain. Hoops awakened Javala. "We're here earlier than expected. The whole stretch of beach appears deserted. I did not see any sign of life as we approached—no campfire smoke, nothing." Javala sprang to her feet, donned her vest, and shouldered her bow and quiver. She smoothed back a cascade of red hair from over her ears and secured it into a ponytail with a leather thong. Hoops noticed that she wore a single gold earring. He recognized it at once.

"I found the mate to your earring back on the island," he said, fumbling at the drawstring to the leather bag at his belt.

Javala laughed. "I lost it when I was searching for bits of driftwood. It is not a fine piece by your Wiffin standards. But, please, keep it, Hoops, as a token of my appreciation. Perhaps, it will bring you luck. Who knows, you may need it!"

She stepped into the calm, knee-high water and waded to the beach. From the water's edge, she called back to Hoops, "How do you catch those green rock fish you are chasing?"

"With long trailing nets."

Javala burst into laughter. "I don't know what your game is, Wiffin, but next time, if you want to convince anyone you're on a fishing expedition, I suggest you bring along some of your nets." She blew him a kiss and, still chuckling, disappeared over the sand dune.

Chapter 6

"I can't imagine anything so dumb as to forget to bring fishing nets," Zaggie growled at Hoops, as he cut bundles of marsh grass to camouflage their boat. It was moored in a narrow tributary of the Black River, out of sight from the sea. "What if we had been boarded by a Sarien patrol vessel? What would you have told them? That we were just on a pleasure cruise?"

"My grandfather specifically told you to help me prepare for this mission," Hoops barked back at the cat. "Why didn't you remember the nets? After all, you're the one who came up with this fishing tale to explain our presence this far south in Sarien waters if we were challenged. I don't want to hear another word from you on this subject. That's an order!"

Satisfied that his craft was properly hidden, Hoops led Havoc and Zaggie through the marshes flanking the river's mouth until they reached the wide stretch of sandy beach bordering the sea. They headed south, back toward the spot Javala had gone ashore almost two leagues away.

Hoops waded along the edge of the beach in ankle-deep water. He didn't want to leave any footprints in the sand that might be traced back to his boat. Much to his dislike, he was forced to carry Zaggie so she wouldn't get wet. Havoc trailed along in the calm water, although occasionally he would wander out on the dry sand to sniff at a dead sea turtle or relieve himself on a bleached piece of driftwood. *Scattered wolf prints on the beach*, Hoops thought. *Should not be alarming to any Sarien legionnaires patrolling the coastline.* So he didn't scold the wolf often.

Twilight was approaching when Hoops decided to turn inland about a half league from where Javala went ashore. Hoops put Zaggie down, and the three of them scampered up a high dune overlooking the beach. They reached the crest of the dune only to be greeted by five fully armed Sarien legionnaires. The legionnaires seemed as surprised at the encounter as Hoops. For a moment, no one said anything. Finally, the tallest, most battle-scarred of the five soldiers broke the silence.

"I am Captain Gartho of the Queen's Fourth Legion. And who might be you?"

"I am Hoops, a shipwrecked Wiffin fisherman. And these are my companions. We are delighted to meet you. Perhaps you can direct us to some seaside village where we can find food and shelter?"

"Perhaps. But first, tell me where you lost your vessel, Wiffin." Captain Gartho had lost two fingers on his left hand. A livid scar ran from the corner of one of his hard black eyes to his upper lip.

"Out at sea, Captain. We encountered a sea serpent. We drifted ashore on flotsam a little ways up the beach," Hoops said, pointing northward.

"Those sea serpents can be nasty," muttered one of the five soldiers. "They wrecked one of our biggest warships last winter. Remember, Captain?"

The captain ignored the comment. "Have you seen anyone along this beach since you landed, Wiffin?"

"No, sir."

"A girl, maybe?"

"We've seen no one along this stretch of beach." *It wasn't a complete lie,* Hoops thought.

"Except for your boots, you don't look wet. Neither does that wolf cowering behind you nor the weird-looking cat. Please explain."

Before Hoops could think up a reply, a score of legionnaires on horseback thundered into view.

"That must be the Lord General himself," Captain Gartho told his men. "He's in a hurry. He must have important news."

General Itus reigned in his massive horse just short of the captain. "Great tidings!" he announced in a gravelly voice. "We have captured the Gretien girl. Already, she is on her life's final journey to the City of Sar and the pit of vipers."

Hoops fought back a wave of nausea.

The general was the biggest man he'd ever seen. His entire face was etched with battle scars. His right hand consisted of a massive iron claw complete with sharpened talons instead of fingers. He jerked off his bronze helmet, and Hoops noticed his right ear had been sliced away. His hard, jet black eyes fell on Hoops.

"What have we here?" he demanded of Captain Gartho.

"A shipwrecked Wiffin fisherman with some strange companions," the captain replied and then repeated what little information Hoops had given him.

The general grunted. "The girl came ashore, presumably from a boat. We know that because we retraced her footprints to the water's edge. I doubt very much she swam to shore from nowhere."

"What's her explanation?" Gartho asked the general.

"She refuses to say anything. But she will be telling us everything she knows and then some after a few hours in the Chamber of Torments with our friendly little inquisitor, Scotus."

Again, Hoops felt nauseous.

Itus circled his horse around Hoops, examining him closely. "Put a rope around the Wiffin's neck and haul him and those silly creatures back to Sar," he growled at the captain. "I distrust his story. He may be another candidate for the Chamber of Torments. Perhaps, the viper pit as well."

When Gartho approached with a rope, Hoops threw up on the captain's polished boots. That brought a burst of laughter from the other soldiers, but one stern glance from Gartho quieted them. "Let's get moving immediately," he shouted. In a quieted tone, he said to Hoops, "Fear not, Wiffin. Just stick to your story when you go before Queen Saragata. Unlike the Lord General, she's not keen on unnecessary torture."

But the sick feeling in Hoops's stomach lasted almost the entire journey to Sar. At one point during their trip, Captain Gartho mounted his horse and rode ahead to consult with General Itus whose unit was well in advance of Gartho's men. He soon returned and dismounted, reporting he had seen the Gretien prisoner and had received orders from Itus to escort the Wiffin to the palace immediately upon reaching the city.

Night settled over the hilly land and storm clouds rolled in, blotting out the moonlight. Gartho marched once again on foot. He had put Zaggie astride his mare. Havoc was led on a leash by a legionnaire.

They topped a final hill to see the sprawling City of Sar below, its back to the vast stretch of water, Dark Harbor. The city was aglow with lights.

"Is the city always lighted up like this?" Hoops asked Gartho, who strolled at his side, loosely holding the free end of Hoops's tether.

"There are always some lights, especially around the palace. But these are the final days of the month of Tor, and the city's festivities are reaching their peak."

"Why all the festivities, Captain?"

"Queen's orders. Tor is the only month when the God of War, Brutius, comes down from the Eternal Mountain to be among us. He likes big parties, and Queen Saragata arranges them in his honor. A waste of the realm's tax money, in my humble opinion."

"Why do you say that, Captain?"

"Never mind my reasons. I've said too much already. I don't want to risk upsetting any of the gods, even that character, Brutius."

They paraded down the hillside and entered the walled city by the main gate. The narrow cobblestone streets were jammed with people of all descriptions. Some were tall and wore armor. Others were diminutive and jostled about almost naked despite the night's chill. Torches lined the streets and charcoal braziers, where vendors were grilling aromatic meats and fish, stood at every corner. The air was heavy with the mingled fragrances of rare spices. The shops were beehives of activity. Hoops imagined that there was nothing in the entire world, from silks to elaborately designed knives and swords to exotic fruits and vegetables, that couldn't be purchased in the bustling city.

It was the different types of people and their radically different clothing that intrigued Hoops the most. "Are all these people Sariens?" he asked Gartho.

The captain grinned. "They are subjects of the queen, if that's what you mean. But few are true native Sariens born in this city and in the countryside immediately surrounding us." Without breaking stride, the officer pointed to a tall, skinny individual with a face painted indigo blue and wearing a gold-striped blue robe that flowed to the ground. "That's a Bodo. He's from a desert tribe in the far south of the kingdom. He'd just as soon cut my throat as smile at me, but he owes allegiance to the queen and he knows that, as a legionnaire, I represent the throne. So he's made up his mind to smile at me instead of putting his dagger to my neck."

"Why such a strong allegiance to the queen, Captain?"

"Because only she holds this kingdom together. We call her the warrior queen. Our kingdom, as long as it stays united, can keep the everpresent enemy, the Lughs, from across the Harbor from overrunning this entire land and enslaving the whole population. Mark my words, Wiffin. If it wasn't for everyone's fear of the Lughs and their respect for our warrior queen as leader, the various clans and tribes would go back to their old ways of killing each other at every opportunity. There would be no kingdom of Sar. Only the God of Anarchy and the Lughs would reign. That's why it's sometimes necessary to punish clans that rebel, like the Gretiens. We can't tolerate disunity here."

"But the Gretien chief wanted to discuss terms. Instead, General ltus staged a surprise attack and slaughtered them. Apparently, for no reason."

Captain Gartho stopped dead and yanked Hoops's off the ground with the rope. Hoops choked.

"Where did you hear that, little Wiffin?" the legionnaire hissed. Then just as abruptly, he let Hoops go. "I know where you heard that tale. If that girl was cleaned up and dressed properly, she'd prove a winsome lassie, no doubt. She could probably convince you to act against your good judgment. So be it, Hoops. But heed my words, be very careful what you say when the queen questions you. A slip like that could cost you dearly. The penalty for aiding and abetting a traitor in this kingdom, whether you're a Wiffin or not, is death. Understand?"

Hoops, rubbing his throat, nodded meekly.

As they neared the palace, Gartho suddenly stepped to a food vendor on a corner, tossed the man a piece of silver, and snatched up a skewer of grilled sardines wrapped in grape leaves. He handed it to Hoops. "Better eat now. You might spend your first evening in a palace dungeon which isn't famed for its culinary arts."

Against the complaints from his squeamish stomach, Hoops readily wolfed down the fish. Meanwhile, the food vendor raced up to Gartho demanding more money. The burly legionnaire ignored the vendor at first, but when man vehemently insisted, Gartho called him a thief and knocked him to the ground with a sidearm blow, much to the amusement of onlookers. They marched into the palace between immense marble statues of legionnaire guards bearing golden spears. Gartho's men with Hoops, Havoc, and Zaggie in tow, tramped along a lengthy corridor floored with colorful marble inlays. Flaming torches from sconces high on ornately decorated walls lighted the way to the massive bronze doors of the throne room.

The doors swung open, and the group walked into the midst of a raucous party. Long banquet tables groaned under the weight of countless silver platters piled high with food of all sorts. Wine flowed everywhere. Hoops noted that the crowd of guests wore either crimson red or spotless white robes, although a few of the revelers had managed to spill red wine over themselves. Between the laughter and loud talking and efforts of three meandering troupes of musicians, the noise was deafening. Intricately carved marble fountains, which Hoops knew to be the work of the Wiffin sculptor Fargo, were scattered about the expansive chamber. The cascading water from these fonts only added to the din. At the far end of the room, where Gartho was leading Hoops, sat the queen on a gold throne. Instead of a royal scepter in her right hand, Saragata gripped a sword with a handle encrusted with glittering jewels. Her raven hair flowed to her waist. She was adorned in purple gowns. She fingered a purple silk handkerchief in her left hand. Before her, in chains, stood a defiant Javala.

"She's a traitor without doubt, Your Majesty," General Itus was concluding, as Gartho and Hoops approached. "She killed three of my legionnaires and seriously wounded another, even after we pleaded with her to surrender. She would have done more damage if she had not exhausted her quiver of arrows, and we were finally able to overcome her."

"What have you to say to these multiple charges brought against you by the Lord General?" the queen asked Javala.

Javala said nothing.

"Please, girl, save yourself additional grief." The queen paused to cough into the handkerchief. "You know that I must condemn you to death for treason. But I can arrange that death be quick and less painful if I so desire. But I need you to answer the few questions we already have put to you."

Javala was steadfast in her silence.

Hoops felt the urge to speak out in Javala's defense. He remembered Captain Gartho's warning and suppressed that urge. It was possible, he reasoned, that Javala had lied to him about the attack on the Gretiens. Maybe it was the Gretiens who attacked first. In any case, he was on a vital mission for Horn Harbor and nothing must stand in the way of that.

"Do we have to ruin a wonderful feast tonight with a trial? Can't we postpone this sordid affair until the morrow?" The speaker was a tall individual with a well-trimmed black beard and a pained look on his face. He, too, was dressed in purple. He stood to one side of the throne, holding a huge silver wine goblet in his hand and looking a shade unsteady on his feet. Hoops guessed this was Brutius, the God of War.

"I suggest, Itus, that we should bow to our guest of honor's request," said Saragata. "This is not the time nor place for a trial of treason. If you think it necessary, I will order her bound over to little Scotus for a few hours in the Chamber of Torments to determine the truth. But that, too, can wait until the morning."

"Oh, let me have fun tonight!" quipped a gnome-like creature with a dirty white beard and beady red eyes. "I have branding irons already heating on the brazier and oil simmering over the fire. This afternoon my assistants installed a brand-new drive mechanism in the rack. We can pull arms and legs out of their sockets in half the time it used to take." Scotus was bouncing with enthusiasm.

"Quiet, Scotus," the queen snapped. "I shall decide the girl's fate but I will do so tomorrow, not during tonight's festivities." She ordered guards to take Javala to the dungeons. Then, she turned her attention to Hoops.

"Who's this?" She wanted to know. "Why does he have a rope around his neck? He looks like a Wiffinvolk, and they always are our guests, Itus, unless there is good reason not to treat them as such."

"He claims he is a fisherman and was shipwrecked near our coast by a sea serpent," explained the lord general. "He says he landed on the beach with his wolf and that strange, catlike creature about a league from where we know the girl came ashore, presumably from a boat. I suggest the Wiffin's story is fishy at best. I also suggest he was aiding the Gretien in some fashion, although he told my men he had not seen her."

"I admit I never heard of a Wiffin fisherman, but then there is a lot I don't know about the Wiffinvolk," the queen said calmly. "If he says he never met the Gretien girl, why should we take argument with him, Itus?"

The queen directed her next question to Hoops. "Tell me, Wiffin. Did you or did you not tell my men that you had not met the girl prisoner?"

"That is precisely what I told them, Your Majesty." It wasn't a total lie. Hoops heard Captain Gartho beside him inhale deeply.

The queen ordered Captain Gartho to remove the rope around Hoops's neck and steer the Wiffin to a banquet table. She demanded meat for a famished Havoc and was about to call for a plate of fish for Zaggie when Brutius interrupted.

"The cat is most unusual and interests me greatly, Your Highness. May I ask that the creature join us at our table as my guest?"

"As you wish, Brutius."

Gartho was about to lead Hoops to a table when Itus called out to the legionnaire, "Did you search the Wiffin?"

"Of course, General. He carried only a stubby belt ax and a hunting knife."

For an instant, Itus seemed satisfied with the reply and began to walk away. He abruptly spun about and demanded of Hoops, "What is in that pouch on your belt?"

"Flint and steel and a tinder box. Maybe a few coins. That's all."

"Hand me the pouch, immediately, or I'll take it from you myself."

With trembling fingers, Hoops removed the pouch and handed it to the general. While Itus was opening the pouch, Hoops uttered a short but sincere prayer to Zob. The chamber became silent as the General Itus's claw hand dug into the pouch and emerged with a gold earring dangling from a steel talon.

In a triumphant voice, Itus announced, "I know who wears the match to this earring. This only proves that this Wiffin and the traitor girl, Javala, have crossed paths, as I suspected. I don't know the extent of his involvement with the girl, but I intend to find out. I suggest to Her Majesty that this Wiffin and our dear Scotus have a little chat in the chamber come daylight."

A grim-faced Queen Saragata reluctantly nodded in agreement.

Chapter 7

Hoops was jarred out of his nightmare-riddled sleep by the grinding of rusty bolts on the dungeon door. He leaped off his bed of moldy straw and stepped barefooted on a squealing black rat. The door swung open to reveal the God of War with torch in hand and a purring Zaggie cradled in one arm. Behind Brutius stood Queen Saragata.

"May we come in?" Brutius inquired cheerfully.

"Please do," replied Hoops. "But watch out for my furry little cell mates."

The god and the queen entered the dank, windowless cell, carefully sidestepping scurrying rats while Hoops struggled back into his boots. For an instant, Hoops thought of drawing his concealed boot knife and trying to bluff his way out of the dungeon with the little weapon. Neither the queen nor Brutius appeared to be armed. But Hoops dismissed the idea. There were bound to be guards in the narrow dungeon corridor. Besides, Hoops had no idea what a Sarien god was capable of doing. Brutius might make the knife melt in Hoops's hand or perform some other magical stunt to render him powerless. Then Hoops would find himself in more trouble than he was in already.

"I have decided the fate of the Gretien girl, Javala," the queen announced solemnly. "She will be beheaded at dawn. I have no other choice when dealing with traitors. It will be a quick death, however, unlike lowering her into the pit of vipers, as Itus recommended, or burning her at the stake which was Scotus's choice. It's a shame to have to put her to death. I could have used a young lady so talented with a bow and arrow."

"Now the queen must decide your fate, Hoops," said Brutius. He had a smug look on his face.

"I've done nothing wrong," Hoops protested.

"We remain convinced that you somehow aided the rebel girl," Brutius said. "You had one of her earrings. You claimed your vessel sank in deep water, and you floated ashore on some of the boat's planking. We don't accept that story. The Great Sarien current would have taken you out to sea, not to our shore. We are convinced the girl landed here by boat. Admittedly, we have not found your ship. But then, neither have we found any pieces of wreckage washed up on the shoreline. In sum, my dear Wiffin, there are several unresolved issues here. As much as I dislike Scotus—he prefers his beef burnt to a cinder and can't distinguish a vintage wine from vinegar—I do believe that you and he should have a little chat in his specially designed chamber."

"I don't have much choice but to resolve this matter quickly and firmly," said the queen. "Many of my guests at the party are aware that you, Hoops, might be involved with Javala, thanks to our overly dramatic General Itus. If, indeed, you have given aid to the traitor girl, then you must die, too. I cannot let word circulate among my subjects that I violate my own laws and allowed anyone involved in treason to go unpunished. I hope you appreciate my position."

Hoops started to protest once more, but the queen cut him short with an authoritative wave of her hand.

"But we now have a new development, thanks to your colleague, Zaggie. She has presented us with a most interesting proposition. If we all agree to it, her plan calls for keeping you alive and in excellent health. Unfortunately, this still leaves me with the problem of dealing with the treason charges against you."

"What proposition? Zaggie, you tell me what this is all about," Hoops said.

Zaggie had a bemused, self-satisfied expression in her yellow eyes. "Of course. I simply told Her Majesty that she should allow you and me, and of course, that silly wolf to continue our trek to

Dourghoul Keep. We will retrieve the notorious talisman from the great witch, Tajine, and bring it back here to Her Majesty. In return for our services to the kingdom of Sar, your life will be spared. You and the wolf will be allowed to return home, if that is still your wish."

"You traitor!" screamed Hoops. "You have betrayed our mission. You have betrayed me. You have betrayed my grandfather. You have betrayed all of Wiffinvolk! You rotten little deformed cat!" Hoops started to reach for his boot knife. He felt the urge to cut Zaggie's throat no matter the consequences.

"I warn you! Don't do anything rash, Hoops," Brutius growled. The god's eyes narrowed and glowed crimson in the flickering torchlight.

Hoops slowly brought his right hand back to his side. He felt tightness in his chest, his breathing labored. For a few seconds, no one spoke. Then Hoops yelled again, "What do you expect to get out of this deal, you traitor?"

"An emerald collar of Wiffin craftsmanship and a senior position in Her Majesty's pet household."

"You'd betray us all for a piece of jewelry and a fancy cat bed? You are disgusting, Zaggie!"

"No need to be abusive to this dear cat," chimed in Brutius. He was smiling now. His eyes had returned to their normal cobalt blue. "Zaggie has taken steps to spare you a lot of pain, perhaps even death. I think you should be grateful to her, instead of calling her names."

"I agree with Brutius," the queen said. "She has not betrayed your country. Zaggie says your wizard grandfather, Armarugh, advised you I would turn my army on Wiffinvolk and enslave the whole lot of you, Wiffins, once I've rid myself of the Lughs. That is a lie. I am against slavery. I'm taking steps to eradicate it in this kingdom. Besides, I treasure Wiffin expertise and talents. I can't imagine your great designer, Haro, creating something this magnificent if it wasn't for money in his purse." She flashed an enormous ruby and emerald ring at Hoops.

"I have sent numerous envoys to the witch, Tajine," continued the queen. "Pleading with her to give the talisman to me rather than risk having it fall into Lugh hands when she dies. I know that she is half Wiffin, and I've made it clear to her that no harm will ever befall the Wiffinvolk as long as I live."

She paused to cough into her handkerchief. "Until Zaggie explained your mission, I had no idea what Tajine intended to do with the talisman. I still don't understand her reasoning for insisting Armarugh gets it for safekeeping. But that is not of paramount importance at the moment. What is important is that if Sar and the Lughs must battle over Dourghoul Keep and the Lughs prove victorious and secure the talisman, the fates of both my kingdom and your homeland will be sealed forever! Do you understand me, Hoops?"

"I do not believe my grandfather would lie to me about a matter as serious as this."

"Apparently, he did," said Zaggie. "You have heard the queen's promise. If you succeed in bringing the talisman to her, no harm will befall Wiffinvolk. If you don't agree to help her, then who knows what will happen? Even with Brutius's help, there is no guarantee the Lughs won't win the battle for Dourghoul Keep. And we all know what that means. Must I remind you that all Lughs are warriors? All they know about is fighting. They depend entirely on slaves to do everything else."

"Do you expect me to walk into Tajine's castle and tell her that I, Armarugh's grandson, am no longer loyal to him, that I intend to give you the talisman instead?" Hoops asked Saragata.

"No, I don't. I do not know how her illness has affected her thinking. Perhaps, common sense is no longer a factor in her decision-making. On the contrary, I expect you to say nothing about me. Let her believe the talisman will be delivered to Armarugh as she wishes. Otherwise, she might decide against giving it to you. In that case, she'll most probably try to hide it somewhere in her castle. But it will be recovered once she's dead. Trust me on that! You then had best pray to the heavens that it will end up in my hands, not in the Lughs'."

"Maybe she'll simply destroy the talisman," Hoops said.

"She can't," commented Zaggie. "That particular talisman has some unusual features. It can only be used once, then it becomes worthless and can be destroyed. But until its power has been unleashed against an enemy, the talisman is indestructible.

"But let me add to what the queen has told you," continued the cat. "If the Lughs recover it, our mission will have been in vain. On the other hand, if you do as Her Majesty commands, our mission won't be a failure. Instead, the ultimate outcome for Wiffinvolk will be the same as if we had been successful in spiriting the talisman away undetected and handing it to your grandfather."

"This all sounds very logical to me," said Brutius. "I can't imagine your grandfather faulting you for saving your country, even if it wasn't exactly according to the plan he had in mind."

Hoops had to admit that the queen and even the treacherous Zaggie were making sense. Besides, under the current circumstances, he didn't see how he had much choice but to agree with them. What if his grandfather had not been totally truthful with him in the first place? Did his grandfather and the dying Tajine have some hidden agenda? He was still furious with Zaggie for having revealed their mission. He wanted to buy more time to consider the plan carefully before he committed himself.

"I'll consider your proposition," Hoops told the queen.

"You best consider it quickly," the queen snapped. "Time is of the essence. Assuming good judgment gets the better of you and you agree to our proposal, I still have to deal with the problem of the charges against you. I cannot ignore those charges, not when everybody in the realm probably has heard about them by now."

"May I suggest a rather simple solution?" announced Zaggie. "Let it be known that, after a few hours in the Chamber of Torments, nothing came out of the interrogation, suggesting that Hoops did any more than stumble across that earring by accident. And there's truth in that."

"But Scotus will know that's not true," the queen replied.

"Please, Your Majesty! You are the queen here! Of course, there will be no interrogation. All you have to do, Your Highness, is tell that slimy Scotus you'll have his legs jerked out of their sockets on his own rack if he breathes a word about this. Rest assured, he'll keep his mouth shut."

"Now that we've solved that problem," exclaimed Brutius. "I suggest we get out of this horribly damp room. If I stay much longer, I'll probably catch a nasty cold which will simply ruin the last few days of this wonderful visit to your city, Your Majesty."

That comment was followed by a curse, as the god kicked away a rat that had started chewing on one of his sandals.

"I still have an unresolved problem," said the queen. "What guarantee do I have that this young Wiffin will bring me the talisman and not try to flee my country with it? I have learned the hard way not to accept someone's promise at face value, especially when that someone apparently has lied to me once already."

Zaggie replied, "I would recommend that some of your trusted legionnaires, perhaps even with General Itus in charge, accompany us to Dourghoul and back here as an insurance measure for you and as a safety measure for us."

"I can send Captain Gartho's Fourth Legion," the queen noted.

"May I be so bold, Your Majesty, to advise you against sending a whole legion," said Zaggie. "Tajine may still have spies. If she learned that an entire legion was marching toward her castle, she might take alarm and do something drastic, provided her illness has not sapped her of all her powers. Instead, I strongly recommend that you send no more than a score or two of soldiers. Tajine would interpret such a small group as just a routine Sarien patrol out on a security mission. For example, scouring the countryside for bandits."

"I agree with Zaggie, Your Highness," Brutius told the queen. "The witch Tajine may be on her deathbed, but we don't know the current extent of her ability to cause mischief. It might be greater than we think. We shouldn't risk upsetting her unnecessarily."

The queen nodded, then coughed again into her handkerchief.

"So we all have agreed on the plan!" Brutius exclaimed. "Excellent! Now let's venture forth into some fresh, dry air before I become ill. This place is dreadfully unhealthy."

"I haven't agreed to anything yet," Hoops said.

"Don't be tiresome, Hoops," hissed Zaggie. "You have few options open to you at this moment."

"I'd like to point out, Hoops," the queen said. "That Scotus is often overly zealous in his work. I regret to say many of his prisoners—innocent or not—never survive the interrogation. If you do not agree with my proposal this instant, you and Scotus will have that little chat. In that case, may the heavens help you. I won't."

Zaggie was right, Hoops thought. He didn't have any options open. The queen's threatening remarks about Scotus's zeal only heightened his uneasiness. His stream of thoughts was interrupted by Zaggie.

"One thing that does worry me, Your Highness, is the time factor," the cat said. "We know Tajine's death is imminent. As mentioned at dinner, only hours ago, you learned that the Lughs already have assembled a large force, presumably to set out for her castle the moment they hear the witch is dead. If I recall my geography correctly, the Lughs are closer to Dourghoul Keep than we are. If we have to journey to the castle by way of the eastern slope of Gauntlet Mountain, it will take us many days to get there. In the meantime, Tajine might die, and the Lughs could get to Dourghoul before us."

"But if you travel west of the mountain, you have to journey through the Great Mire, and worse, the land of the fierce Skaggs," Saragata replied. "Such a small number of my legionnaires, as you've proposed, would have no chance if it came to a battle with hordes of Skaggs with their poison darts."

"I agree, Your Highness," said the cat. "But we'll have to take that risk. Hopefully, we can cross Skagg territory without meeting any sizable force of those little horrors."

"I think your suggestion is stupid, Zaggie." Hoops said. "You're not only a traitor, but you seem intent on getting us all killed."

"Well, Hoops, if you're so much smarter, let's hear your proposal as to how we can cross Skagg territory safely," retorted the winged feline.

Hoops was surprised. Why did Zaggie challenge him to find a solution? What was she up to now? Zaggie didn't do anything without a reason.

Suddenly, he remembered Javala's remarks about baby Skaggs. "If we want to get through the land of the Skaggs without a fight, then I suggest you take along a safe passage ticket. You have one right here in your dungeons."

"What are you talking about, Wiffin?" snorted Brutius.

"I am talking about the Gretien girl, Javala. She's accepted by the Skaggs. She even knows the Skagg leader, Yukman. Use her as a hostage, if you will, and I bet the Skaggs will decide, however reluctantly, to let us pass unharmed through their lands. Javala can save you time and lives."

"By Zob," uttered a grinning Zaggie. "What a brilliant idea, Hoops! I wish I had thought of that."

"But I cannot simply let that traitor go free, even if it's only for the duration of this mission," said Saragata.

"I hate to say it, Your Majesty, but I don't think you have many options open at this point," Hoops replied. "I'm sure you can dream up some excuse for her absence at the chopping block at dawn."

"What if the stubborn girl refuses to accompany you on this journey and in her misplaced pride, elects instead to be a martyr for her clan's cause?" asked Brutius.

"Just put her in chains and drag her along, if necessary," replied Zaggie. "I'm sure General Itus can handle her. Unless," and she chuckled. "She somehow gets her hands on a bow and arrow. If that happens, I'm afraid Her Majesty may find herself looking for a new general."

Brutius cursed again. This time a rat had found a big toe exposed and bit into it. "Please, let us finish this conversation somewhere else. That beast really hurt!"

Hoops shook his head. "Before I agree to do anything, there are a few loose ends I want settled right now."

"Now, what?" asked the frustrated God of War. He turned to the queen. "Must this Wiffin be part of the operation? He's so negative!"

"I thought we made it clear, Brutius. Tajine will only surrender the talisman to Armarugh's personal representative. That's our Hoops." There was a clear note of exasperation in the queen's voice.

"So be it," muttered a disgusted Brutius.

"What still has to be resolved, Wiffin?" The queen was irritated now.

"I suggest that only the four of us in this room know the true purpose of the journey to Dourghoul Keep. It's for security reasons. The talisman obviously represents great power for its possessor. If one of your overly ambitious legionnaires, Itus, for example, suddenly suffers visions of great personal power and glory, he might be tempted to steal it on the way back here."

"Itus already knows the true purpose of your journey. He was privy at the banquet table when Zaggie broached the subject," said Saragata. She hesitated a few seconds, then said, "General Itus is trustworthy."

"That's too bad because I don't think he is," Hoops replied.

"I beg your pardon, little Wiffin," the queen snapped back. "Itus commands my army, but I command him. I decide who's to be trusted in this realm. Don't you forget that!"

Hoops ignored her anger. For some reason, he suddenly felt sure of himself. For once, he seemed to be holding some winning cards.

"The second item I want settled now is the fate of Javala after she returns to Sar. I want her spared the death penalty."

The queen drew back her arm as if to strike him but didn't follow through. Instead, she glared at Hoops, coughed, and said in a hoarse voice, "For someone who, only a short while ago, was facing the Chamber of Torments and possibly death, you demand a great deal of me."

"Well? Do you grant the request or not?" Hoops insisted.

"May I interject something, Your Highness?" said Zaggie in a diplomatic tone. "I am certain that Your Majesty could decide on some punishment other than death for the girl. You could decree, for example, that she acted only in self-defense or that she is too young to really understand treason and all its implications. A life in prison might satisfy your subjects' desire for justice. Or maybe just a severe public flogging would appease them."

"I begrudgingly agree to spare her the death penalty upon her return here, Wiffin," replied the queen. "But that's provided she behaves herself during this mission. No trouble of any kind, understand?"

Hoops nodded.

"Agreed then," said Saragata. "By the way, Hoops, I'll be getting a full report about her behavior from Itus himself. Remember that."

So much for my efforts to save the girl, thought Hoops. But he decided it was best to say nothing further, at least, for the time being.

Chapter 8

At daybreak, the column marched out of the City of Sar into a dim world of swirling wet snow. The giant General Itus, mounted on his gigantic stallion, led the march. Close behind came Captain Gartho on foot beside his mount, with Zaggie clinging to the horse's saddle. Hoops trudged along beside the captain. Twenty-two soldiers from Gartho's Fourth Legion followed in single file. At the rear were the supply packhorses, one of which also carried Javala. A bulky soldier named Var, one of Itus's personal guards, marched alongside Javala's mount. He was holding fast to the end of an iron chain linked to a brass collar around the girl's slender neck. Havoc trotted beside Javala.

Hoops had not been able to speak with Javala since the girl had been dragged off to the dungeons the night before. Itus had seen to it that the two were kept separated.

"I don't want those two getting together and hatching a plot against us," Hoops overheard the Lord General say to Saragata. The general also insisted that Javala's hands be bound throughout the journey, but the queen had replied, "Surely, Var is capable of controlling that slip of an unarmed girl with just a chain around her neck. There is no reason to make her more miserable than necessary."

The queen had ordered Javala bathed and her garments cleaned. "A harsh winter has settled in, and I see no reason why the Gretien prisoner should risk getting a cough like the one that's plagued me for so long," she told her servants in front of Hoops. She ordered them to provide Javala with a hooded white ermine cloak from her own wardrobe.

As they sloshed along in the fast accumulating snow, Gartho muttered to Hoops, "Nasty weather for so early this winter. The gods must be frowning. Perhaps they know this mission, whatever it is, is an ill-fated one. Do you know what we're doing, Hoops?"

"What did General Itus tell you?"

"When I asked him about this mission, he told me to keep my mouth shut and obey orders. But he did say something about heading north, past Gauntlet Mountain. But what really puzzles me," the captain continued. "Is why we are dragging that Gretien girl along, and you and your talking cat."

Hoops pulled his woolen cowl more tightly about his head and walked on in silence.

"Reckon, you're not going to tell me, Hoops," Gartho said with a sigh. "Reckon, I'll find out soon enough."

Hoops would have been more comfortable having Gartho, not Itus, aware of the mission's goal, but he recalled he was the one who insisted knowledge of the mission be strictly limited. Unfortunately, that was before he'd been told Itus was privy to the information. Hoops toyed with the idea of giving Gartho some inkling of what was going on, but he decided that might be too risky. The outspoken captain might inadvertently let slip to Itus what he knew. Hoops changed the subject. "Captain, I noticed your legionnaires don't have plumes adorning their helmets. I also noticed that your men all carry swords and, except for the bowmen, they have javelins but no shields like some of the other legionnaires I saw back in Sar."

"We are men of the Fourth Legion, Wiffin. We wear those silly plumes only when we're on parade. As for shields, they are for defense. The Fourth Legion knows only how to attack the enemy. Does that satisfy your curiosity?"

Hoops muttered a "Yes, sir."

The snow seemed to be falling more heavily by the moment. The low barren foothills ahead were turning a featureless white. The wind picked up, reducing visibility at times to a few paces. The royal highway of smooth paving stones was slick with a thin film of ice beneath the fresh snow. Both men and beasts, except for the loping wolf, Havoc, had to struggle for sure footing. Hoops's bad knee was throbbing from the exertion.

As they began their ascent into the hills, a packhorse lost its footing and slid sideways into a deep drainage ditch. The legionnaire in charge of the horse was able to get the animal back on its feet, but the creature had suffered an injury to one of its front legs and was limping badly. Gartho ordered the legionnaire to lead the animal back to the city after distributing its burdens to the other horses.

An irate Itus countermanded the captain's orders. "I'll not lose time nor men because of an injury to a dumb beast," he shouted. The general drew his sword, reined his steed around, and charged the packhorse. Blood splashed across the snow as Itus severed the beast's head from its body with one blow.

The stunned silence that followed was broken by a piercing scream of rage from Javala.

"Shut that girl up or I'll do the same to her," Itus yelled back to Var. He then ordered the men to strip the dead horse of its burdens, repack them on the remaining animals, and resume marching on the double.

He rode up to Gartho. "No delays. Understand, Captain?" The general's eyes glowered like ice beneath his heavy, snow-flecked brows. "If we hurry up this motley crowd, we might have time to stop for a quick meal in Vecka before we move on northward."

"Why Vecka, General? That's to the west of Gauntlet Mountain. You can't go much further past that hamlet before you run into the Great Mire. We should be traveling eastward if we're going around the mountain."

"Do not dare question my orders, Gartho. I swear that before nightfall, I intend to be at edge of the mire, ready to cross it tomorrow. Now get these troops moving!"

The General spurred his horse forward and disappeared into a flurry of snow ahead of the column. Gartho didn't move at first. Hoops could read a mixture of anger and fear in the captain's eyes. At last, the captain muttered aloud to no one in particular, "May the deities save us all. The Great Mire, no less. We are doomed!"

He regained his composure and began barking orders in every direction. The march resumed. Over the foothills, the snow tapered off, but the clouds remained low and threatening. The band descended into a wide valley of snow-covered grazing land sparsely dotted by stonewalled hovels with thatched roofs. Wisps of pale gray smoke from cooking fires hung over some of them, but most were obviously abandoned.

A sad and dreary landscape, Hoops thought. Gartho must have been thinking the same, for he said quietly, "This was once a thriving valley with great herds of livestock. Then a strange disease struck the herds, and now look at it. A pitiful sight, this valley."

"I wonder if it was the same disease that struck the herds in the Gretien lands? Javala said their herds have been devastated by disease."

Gartho shrugged his broad shoulders. "Perhaps only the Goddess of the Herdsmen knows for sure, and she hasn't said a thing to me." He chuckled softly. "I don't think she has any intention of telling me anything. I'm just a dumb soldier. I'm only supposed to converse with our God of War and, just between you and me, I think he's a fool. I'm glad the month of Tor is coming to an end in a few days, and Brutius will have to return to the Eternal Mountain somewhere in the heavens for another year. It's my humble opinion that he's a bad influence on our queen. But don't you repeat my words to anyone, Hoops. Promise?"

Hoops nodded. Then he asked the captain, "Why did your men slaughter what was left of the Gretien livestock? Javala swears your troops did that."

Gartho stopped and frowned down at Hoops. "We, of the Fourth Legion, are true professionals. We don't slaughter helpless domestic animals. Itus commanded soldiers from another Sarien legion when he attacked the Gretiens. Neither I nor my men were involved in that affair."

It was late in the afternoon when the tired, cold, and sodden group tramped into Vecka. The hamlet consisted of little more than a few huts in total disrepair and a long, low building of rough-hewed logs which served as both a stable and a tavern. Itus dismounted in front of the tavern. Var gave Javala's chain a vicious yank, dragging the girl off her horse. Javala landed facedown in the muddy slush. Havoc snarled and appeared on the verge of lunging at Var, but slunk away when Var threatened him with a drawn sword.

Var burst out laughing, as Javala, in her mud-stained ermine cloak, struggled to her feet. "She's looking less like a princess. More like little, dirty-faced village urchin now." Itus grinned. The other legionnaires glowered at Var. Hoops saw Gartho's right hand instinctively clutch the hilt of his sword. Only when Var turned his back and, dragging Javala behind him, disappeared into the tavern did the captain relax his grip.

The tavern was a narrow room partitioned off from the stable by tattered, grease-stained strips of canvas. The furniture consisted of three battered oaken tables and benches. All the legionnaires, save Gartho, crowded into the cramped space, hoping to find warmth and to escape the sleet that had begun pelting the hamlet. Several paces outside the inn's entrance, an old woman bundled in a dirty, threadbare shawl used a long-handled wooden paddle to stir the contents of a cauldron suspended from an iron tripod over a bed of coals. Gartho began speaking with her.

As Hoops approached, he heard Gartho haggling over the price of a meal for the entire contingent. The old woman had a bitter, stubborn look in her eyes. No, she wouldn't accept gold from the legionnaire. It was useless in Vecka where there was nothing to buy, no matter how much gold you had. She demanded salt instead. After all, she explained to the exasperated legionnaire, salt had real value.

"The hunter," she said. "Has killed two wild bison to help keep us alive this winter. But the meat has to be cured. We ain't got scant salt to do that."

The captain finally agreed to part with a bag of salt from the contingent's slim food supplies in return for stew for everyone. The old woman flashed a toothless grin of triumph, and Gartho started to return to the inn. Hoops stopped him.

"Captain, can you please make sure Javala gets something to eat? I don't trust that Var character to look after her, and neither Itus nor Var will let me near her."

"Don't worry about her, little Wiffin. I'll see to it that she gets her fill, no matter what Itus and Var wish." He trudged across the thin layer of snow that coated the muddy ground, leaving footprints of brown slush.

Hoops was about to go back inside the tavern but decided against it. The smell of raw manure from the stable permeated the entire structure. Despite the chill that penetrated his damp woolen cloak, he remained outside with a hungry Havoc at his heels. Hoops moved closer to the cooking fire, extending his hands, palms down, toward the coals. At first, the old woman ignored him, her attention riveted on her pot of stew. A young lad, perhaps younger than Hoops, emerged from the tavern with crude earthen bowls on a large wooden tray. The old woman ladled stew into each bowl, and the youth disappeared back into the inn.

Hoops remarked to the old woman, "It smells good, whatever it is."

A wide smile immediately creased her plump face. "You'd best eat some while it lasts, young fella." She picked up a clay bowl lying in the mud next to the fire, spat into it, and then wiped it out with a ragged end of her shawl. She handed it to Hoops. "Spanking clean bowl for ye. Now help yourself. It's bison stew." She glanced over Hoops's shoulder. "Best thank our hunter yonder. He killed 'em in the Great Mire."

Hoops turned around and saw a man sitting on a stump used for splitting kindling. The man wore a long black cloak. A hood shrouded his face, and Hoops could only make out a pair of dark eyes flanking a thin, beaklike nose. He wore black leather gloves and muddied leather boots with a dirt-encrusted big toe protruding through a hole.

"You are the hunter?" Hoops asked.

"Aye, that's me or so the folks around here call me." The man's voice was soft, almost musical. "The old woman's wrong. Those beasts were not in the Great Mire. They were grazing on the edge of that dismal swamp. Few creatures venture into that place. Not much to eat in there. It's all dead. Been that way since back in ancient times. The Great Mire is a strange place, all right. The laws of nature don't apply there."

"Do you ever venture into the Mire?" Hoops asked, as he fed Havoc a chunk of bison from his bowl. The red wolf gulped it down noisily.

"Aye, sometimes. And sometimes, roe deer, which ain't too bright, will venture into the mire. But they rarely come back out."

"The quagmires swallow them?" Hoops asked.

The hunter chuckled softly. "Nay. Roe deer ain't that dumb. They know to avoid the water-filled bogs in there. They even know how to avoid what we call the mire's dry sinkholes. Them's the ones lurk under what looks to me and you like firm, solid ground. But you step into one of them, and you'll be swallowed up faster than it takes a lightning bolt from the heavens to strike the ground. Nay. It ain't the quagmires or the sinkholes that do in the roe deer. It's creatures in the mire that gobble 'em up."

The old woman interrupted. "Now don't you go filling up this poor lad's head with yer tales of Mire creatures." She turned to Hoops. "The hunter here loves to frighten everyone in the village, especially the children, with awful tales about Ghoulvats and other nasty critters that live in the Mire. Don't you pay him too much heed."

Hoops was about to ask the hunter more about the *creatures* when he heard Captain Gartho shout, "We're moving out, Hoops. Get a move on."

The captain was adjusting the saddlebags on his horse. Zaggie was already perched on the saddle. "Itus wants to march at least another league before night."

"You going into the Great Mire?" the hunter said. It was more of a statement than a question.

"We are doing just that," Hoops replied. "But tell me, hunter, how do the deer know when they come upon one of those sinkholes, the ones you called *dry sinkholes?* Those don't exist where I come from."

The hunter chuckled again. "Guess you don't have 'em, Wiffin. Bet they don't exist except in the Great Mire. Anyway, like most wild beasts, the deer stay shy of mushrooms, especially those mushrooms

59

in the Great Mire that look like little red hearts. Beware of them, Wiffin."

"Don't dally around, Hoops. Get a move on," Gartho yelled.

Hoops handed his empty stew bowl to the old woman and thanked her. Then he turned to bid farewell to the hunter. But the hunter wasn't there. "Where did he disappear to so fast?" he asked the old woman. "Who ya talking about, lad?"

"The man who was sitting over there on the stump. The hunter."

The old lady looked puzzled. "The hunter left well before dawn this morning. Ain't seen him since."

Hoops glanced again at the spot where the hunter had been sitting. He realized the coating of snow on the top of the stump was undisturbed. No signs of footprints were visible in the snow around it or even near it. Rattled, Hoops approached Gartho. "Did you see that man I was talking to over there not far from the cooking fire?"

"Been too busy trying to get this crew on the march to notice anything," the captain grumbled.

Hoops looked up at Zaggie. "Didn't you see him?"

"I didn't notice. Guess, I was catnapping," the winged creature replied. She yawned and tried to look disinterested, but her large yellow eyes glimmered with amusement at Hoop's bewilderment.

Chapter 9

Twilight was slithering its way through the overcast sky when the band reached the edge of the Great Mire. The swamp was shrouded with pale gray mist that swirled in and out, as if alive among the long dead, blackened oak trees that jutted up from the mire's floor of dead leaves, broken branches, and acidic-smelling gray-green mold. The legionnaires were a silent crowd. A current of nervousness and uncertainty flowed among them. Only Itus seemed confident.

The general dismounted and ordered Hoops to approach. With Hoops at his side, the leader walked a distance ahead, out of earshot of the soldiers. "Now, little Wiffin, this is your chance to show me how good you are at finding safe passage through this dismal place," the general said. "I don't want to lose man nor beast to some pool of quicksand almost immediately after we set foot in there. The men are edgy enough already. If we have an accident right off, I may have a serious morale problem on my hands. Understand?"

Hoops nodded.

"Once we're into that mire, we're committed and there won't be any choice but to continue on, even if we lose a few souls on the way," Itus said. "But I'm expecting you not to let that happen. If it does, there are going to be serious consequences for you. And that includes your weird cat, that timid wolf, and, oh yes, that Gretien girl, as well. Understand?"

Hoops nodded once more.

"We have a little time left before nightfall. You and I are going to venture into that mire now and seek a safe path for a few hundred paces or so. Then we will return here so the troops can see we are alive and well and there's nothing to fear in that mire. We'll camp back here for the night. At dawn, we'll all march through the Great Mire with bubbling enthusiasm. Right?"

Hoops replied, "But we don't have much time. You don't wander around in a swamp like that in the pitch dark."

"Agreed," said Itus. "One other thing, Wiffin. It's not that I don't trust you, but I have a vague feeling that you don't like me very much. As an added safety precaution, we're going to bring along that Gretien girl with us. She is going to walk in front of me, and I'll have my sword in hand. If something happens, like I'm accidentally led into quicksand or the likes, rest assured, her soul will be in a Gretien hell much earlier than she expected. Do we understand each other, Wiffin?"

Hoops didn't respond. He went off in search of a broken tree limb that could be used as a ground probe. Meanwhile, Itus walked to the rear of the halted column and returned, pushing a sullen Javala ahead of him. Her mud-splattered fur cloak had been left on the packhorse. Itus had removed the brass collar from her neck but her hands were bound behind her back.

"It might be rough going in the mire," Hoops said in disgust. "Sometimes it's difficult to keep your balance with your hands tied up like that."

"If she falls down, so be it. I'll drag her to her feet."

Hoops motioned to Havoc to join them, but Itus shook his head. "That wolf has taken a liking to the Gretien. I saw how it reacted when Var dragged Javala off her horse back in the hamlet. That wolf's timid but I still don't trust him. Not with that girl around."

Taking a deep breath, Hoops stepped through the curtain of mist into the Great Mire. Javala and Itus were immediately behind him. They had gone only a few paces when suddenly the mist opened up directly ahead of them, revealing a tunnellike path weaving its way between the dead trees. The ground was covered with a carpet of rotting leaves and greenish mold. Fallen tree limbs and twigs lay everywhere. They marched in silence. Something was bothering Hoops. At first, he couldn't identify what it was but then realized that twigs and small branches beneath their feet were dry and brittle. Yet the mist pressing about them was like a soggy wall of dirty cotton. With his palm, he felt one of the tree trunks. The flaking bark was dry. It was as if, instead of being in a damp, fog-shrouded swamp, the tree was in the middle of a sun-drenched desert.

The hunter was right, Hoops thought. The Great Mire defied the laws of nature. At length, they came upon large circular pool of scummy black water filled with streamers of brown algae. Hoops walked along the edge of the pool for a short distance, probing the water's depth with his stick. "It's only ankle-deep along here," he told Javala and Itus. "Back home, we have quagmires like this. Sometimes you can wade right across. But sometimes you can step into a bottomless pit of ooze and get sucked down to your death. Best we try to find a way around this one, even if we do lose some time."

"Maybe we should return to the camp now while we still have some light." It was the first time Hoops had heard Javala utter a word since they had left Sar.

"I'll decide when we turn around, girl," snarled Itus. He said something else to the Gretien, but Hoops wasn't listening. He had glanced down at the ground and his attention was suddenly riveted by a thin line of pale red mushrooms sprouting from the leafy mold. They were shaped like little hearts. There were only a few inches from his right foot.

"Keep to your left!" he shouted. But his warning was too late.

A startled Itus took one step too far to the right and immediately sank to his waist in quicksand. The giant man, choking back a scream of surprise mingled with terror, dropped his sword and flung both arms out in front of him, trying to regain solid ground. But it was out of his reach. He began thrashing at the sinkhole's leaf-coated slime. His efforts only encouraged the ooze to suck him down further.

"By the powers, Wiffin, get me out of here!"

Hoops immediately thrust his probing stick out to the general who grabbed it with both hands. "Hold on tightly. I'm going to try to drag you out but you've got to stop struggling, General. That's only making you sink faster."

No sooner had he spoken, Hoops was sent sprawling to the ground by Javala. With hands still bound behind her back, she had slammed into him with her whole body.

"Don't you dare try to rescue that beast!" Javala screamed savagely at Hoops.

The general's eyes were wide with fright, but a torrent of angry obscenities escaped his lips. Itus was still grasping one end of Hoops's probe stick. Hoops scrambled on hands and knees back to the edge of the hole. He reached out and grabbed the loose end of the branch. He was back on his feet when he saw Javala charging him again, this time, with head down like an infuriated bison. Hoops jumped aside and instinctively lashed out with closed fist. His blow landed on the side of her head. She instantly crumpled to the ground, unconscious. "Please, Zob, I pray I didn't hurt her badly," he heard himself saying aloud.

He leaned over her, hand on her throat, searching for a pulse, when Itus began screaming hoarsely, "I'm sinking deeper. By the gods, Wiffin, you've got to help me!" Hoops glanced at the general. Itus now was up to his chest in the quicksand. Hoops immediately left Javala's side and stepped back to the edge of the sinkhole. Once more, he was able to get a solid grasp on the branch to which Itus still clung desperately. Mustering all his strength, Hoops pulled on the stick.

At first, the general didn't budge. The sinkhole refused to surrender its victim. Itus sank another inch. He was now up to his armpits in the morass. For a moment, the general's plight seemed hopeless, and Hoops almost gave up. Itus must have sensed it for he renewed his high-pitched pleas for help. Hoops drew a deep breath and yanked on the stick with all his might. Suddenly, there was a feeling of movement. Itus was several inches closer to the edge of the pit. Hoops stepped backward and sat down, planting his feet firmly in front of him, heels dug into the earth in an attempt to gain more purchase. Once again, he started pulling.

The general began moving inch by slow, painful inch to within an arm's length of firm land. "Now, Itus, reach out with one arm, not both, and see if you can reach the edge." Itus reached forward with his iron hand. Its talons sunk deeply into solid soil at Hoops's feet. The powerful soldier dragged himself to the edge of the sinkhole. Then, using both arms, he heaved himself up out of the slime. An exhausted Hoops collapsed backward on the ground, gasping for breath. He felt dizzy. He closed his eyes for a few moments. The dizziness subsided.

When Hoops reopened his eyes, he saw a towering, mud-smeared Itus standing with his back to Hoops at the edge of the sinkhole. He was holding a limp Javala high over his head like a featherweight, broken doll to be discarded. "Don't you dare, Itus!" Hoops was on his feet instantly, his belt ax drawn. "I swear I'll split you right down the spine if you drop her in there."

Itus turned his head and looked down over his shoulder at Hoops. His lips were twisted in a sardonic grin. "You're threatening me, Wiffin? I sincerely hope not, otherwise, I'll have to rip you apart with this clawed hand of mine."

"No, you won't, Itus. Nor will you toss that girl into the sinkhole. You're not that stupid. You need her and you need me, or else, General, you're going to face the wrath of a very unhappy Queen Saragata when you return without the talisman she so desperately wants."

Itus curled his lips as if to say something, but Hoops cut him off. "I have a feeling that the queen's little Scotus would be delighted with you. You're big and you're strong, so you would last quite a while in his little chamber of torments before you uttered your very last scream."

Itus turned his head and peered down at the sinkhole at his feet. For an agonizing long time, he remained motionless while Hoops prayed to Zob for help. Abruptly, the general turned around and unceremoniously dropped Javala at Hoops's feet. Javala moaned and her eyelids began flickering. Hoops muttered a silent prayer of thanks to Zob.

"Listen to me carefully, Wiffin," Itus said viciously. "You are right about one thing, Hoops. I must obey the queen. At least, for the time being. But once I've done my duty as a soldier and have the talisman in hand, there will be no more use for you or for that Gretien. Do you understand what I'm saying? You have bought yourselves a little more time, but not much more, believe me."

65

Chapter 10

They broke camp at the first hint of a gray dawn. The Great Mire loomed before them; black skeletal trees veiled in a pale, dirty brown mist. The legionnaires said little to one another as they moved about extinguishing cooking fires and packing equipment. The eerie silence of the mire was only broken sporadically by the fluttering wings of a flock of ravens watching them from atop the dead trees.

"Birds of doom, I call them," Captain Gartho muttered, glancing up at the ravens. He was loading his sleeping gear—a rough wool blanket and stuffed goatskin for a pillow—onto his horse. "Many times, I've seen them, Hoops, perched like that near a battlefield, waiting till the slaughter was over. Then they descend to feed on the dead. Sometimes those scavengers start pecking away at men still alive but too wounded to fend them off."

"I get the impression, Captain, that you don't care that much for war."

"Perhaps you're right, Wiffin. War is always tragic. But there are times when there's no choice but to fight. I chose to become a soldier because, I figured, my talents, meager as they may be, could best be used to defend my homeland, and the gods know I've done enough of that."

"I always believed that professional soldiers thought of war in terms of glory and heroics and such."

"Reckon, some do. I bet our God of War does, too. But then Brutius has never been in the front lines of a real battle. He couldn't kill anybody if he tried."

"Why not, Captain?"

"He's a god, sure enough. He can trick you. He can scare you. He can cause you unbearable pain. But kill you? That he can't do. Don't know what your Wiffin deities can do, but we Sariens know that only the Supreme Power, be it a he, she, or it, can give mortals life or take it away."

"Did you always want to be a soldier, Captain?"

"I almost became a farmer like my father, but somehow, spending my life behind a plow wasn't very appealing, especially when I was young like you. But there have been plenty of times since when I wondered if I shouldn't have chosen a plow instead of a sword."

Itus was striding among the men, roaring orders. The general's bronze breastplate and tunic still bore traces of mire slime. Itus had replaced his sword with one confiscated from an archer. The weapon was much smaller than the monster blade he had lost in the sinkhole. In his massive iron claw fist, it looked more like a large hunting knife than a battle sword.

"Be careful how we tread around the Lord General, Hoops. I don't know what really happened in the Great Mire last evening, and I doubt you'll tell me. But no matter. It's just that I haven't seen him this angry in a long time. Losing his favorite sword hasn't helped his disposition. My legionnaires think it might have been you who saved him from a bog or whatever last evening. Whether that's true or not, it's their thinking, and that makes them wonder if the Lord General is as invincible as he's led everyone to believe. I bet the general senses their feelings, and that's really got him furious."

While the troops finished packing gear, Hoops led Havoc a short distance from the camp. From a pocket inside his jerkin, he produced a handful of small red heart-shaped mushrooms and held them out to the wolf. Havoc sniffed them and immediately backed away. "Good," said Hoops in a half whisper. "I'm counting on your keen nose, Havoc. I want you out ahead of us at all times. Agreed?" The wolf flicked his ear to signal he understood.

"Get your legionnaires on the move, Captain. And I mean now!" Itus shouted at Gartho. "I expect to be through the Great Mire by nightfall."

"That's impossible," said Zaggie softly. She was in her usual perch on Gartho's horse. "The Great Mire is too big to cross in one day's time."

"How do you know so much about this swamp, Zaggie?" Hoops asked.

Zaggie seemed amused by the question. "I guess I learned something about the Great Mire from Armarugh. Your grandfather is an avid student of everything. That includes geography."

"Make sure you keep a firm grasp on that chain, Var," Itus yelled. "If that Gretien fiend gets away from you, I'll cut your throat right after I've tracked her down and cut hers."

Hoops glanced over his shoulder. He saw Javala at the rear of the single file formation of legionnaires and packhorses. She was on foot, being led by a grim-faced Var. Javala had not said a word to anyone, including Hoops, since the sinkhole incident. There was not a flicker of expression in her eyes, but Hoops knew rage was boiling behind that blank look. He hoped that rage was directed only at Itus, but he worried some of her wrath might be targeted at himself. After all, he not only had saved the general's life but he had struck down Javala in the process. The purplish bruise on her cheek was visible between strands of uncombed red hair flowing over her shoulders. Hoops uttered a silent prayer to Zob, "Please persuade her to forgive me."

Hoops, probe stick in hand, was the point man in the column when it finally got underway. Havoc was at his side. Gartho, leading his horse with Zaggie astride, followed behind Hoops. The rest of the unit was strung out behind, with Itus on horseback, and Javala and Var along with the packhorses bringing up the rear.

As it did the previous evening, the curtain of clammy mist parted before them once they entered the mire, giving Hoops a clear view of the twisting trail among stark tree trunks. They soon reached the bog that had confronted them earlier, and Hoops gingerly began to move around it. When they reached the place where Itus had stepped into the sinkhole, Hoops was amazed to see that all evidence of that death trap had been erased. The spot again looked like solid ground, covered over with dead vegetation and a smattering of twigs. But the mushrooms were visible, and Havoc instinctively backed away from them. "Good wolf," Hoops whispered. "Keep it up."

A raucous chorus of cawing erupted above their head. The flock of ravens had followed them into the mire. The racket ceased abruptly as soon as the last packhorse in the formation was led past the sinkhole. Hoops wondered if the birds' sudden silence reflected their disappointment that the pit had failed to claim a victim.

With Havoc sniffing the way, they made better time than Hoops had expected. Only twice in as many leagues were they forced to make major detours around large black water bogs. They encountered several mushroom-ringed sinkholes, but between Havoc's keen nose and Hoops's sharp eyes, these were easily detected and avoided. Hoops realized that the presence of those heart-shaped mushrooms held no significance for anyone save himself and the wolf. He decided to keep it that way, at least, for the time being. It was late afternoon before Itus reluctantly allowed the group to halt for a brief rest. Hoops wandered over to where Javala sat on a log, sipping water from a leather container a legionnaire had handed her. Havoc laid at her feet.

Var, with a tight grip on her chain, sat nearby. He glared at Hoops. "My orders are to keep you two from talking. So back away, Wiffin."

"Don't worry, Var," Javala said in a calm, cold tone. "I have nothing to say to this pathetic Wiffin. He betrayed me." She took another sip from the bottle and spat it in Hoops's direction. Hoops backed away.

"Enough loitering. Get off your butts and let's get moving." Itus's roar jarred everyone into motion. "I don't want to be caught in this forsaken mire when night falls."

The men silently formed up in a single file. Havoc rejoined Hoops, and once again, the pair led the way. The silence, like the mist around them, was heavy and oppressive. It was broken only by the periodic flutter of wings as the flock of ravens flew from one treetop to another, tracking the band's movements below. Havoc had been pacing a few yards ahead of Hoops, nose to the ground, when he stopped abruptly, raised his head, ears alert and twitching, and began sniffing about him. Hoops raised his arm to call a halt to the march.

"What's wrong?" asked Gartho who was just behind Hoops. "Wolf smell something?"

Before Hoops could answer, a thin, childlike cry floated at them from somewhere in the mist. That cry was followed by a series of muffled moans.

"Someone's hurt out there," Gartho said in a hushed tone.

The captain's remark was followed by an agonized wail. It sounded close by.

"It's the Ghoulvats. We must be coming too close to the Great Mire's necropolis, and they're not pleased," said Zaggie.

"By Zob, please explain, Zaggie," muttered Hoops. The moans and wails rapidly grew into a chorus all around them. The hairs on the back of his neck prickled. "Who are the Ghoulvats, and what's a necropolis?"

"The Ghoulvats are the tormented souls of the race that once inhabited the Great Mire many millenniums ago. The necropolis is where they are buried. Ghoulvats are spirits. They can't do us real harm, but legend has it that the gods created great monsters to help the Ghoulvats protect their gravesites."

"I must say, Zaggie, for a cat you know a lot more than I would have guessed," said Hoops. "What do you recommend we do now?"

"Change the direction of our march and see if we can't find a way around the necropolis which may be dead ahead, judging from the Ghoulvats' reaction."

"We'll lose time," Gartho pointed out. "Itus won't like it at all."

"You can be certain I won't like it," growled Itus.

Neither he nor Gartho heard the general approach from the rear of the halted column.

"We're not going to waste more time just because of some weird cat's gibberish. A few moans and groans don't frighten me, Wiffin. Guess you've never been on a battlefield littered with the wounded and dying. No detours, Hoops. We're marching straight ahead through this forsaken swamp. I don't want to hear more nonsense from your cat. Understand? Get moving!" The general returned to the rear of the column.

"We are making a serious mistake," muttered Zaggie. "It might prove to be a fatal one."

Chapter 11

Although evening was fast approaching, Itus refused to call a halt. The cries of the Ghoulvats became increasingly louder and harsher. Even Gartho's normally stoic horse was becoming skittish.

"We're getting too close to the burial ground," Zaggie said in low voice. "And I notice the mist seems to be closing in upon us, Hoops."

"She's right about the mist," Gartho told Hoops. "I'm having trouble seeing much past you. No matter what Itus thinks, we'll have to call a halt soon and camp until daybreak."

A piercing scream erupted from the mist just a few paces from them. Instantly, the mire fell silent. The mist opened up before them, revealing a massive mound of moss-covered stones. The mound was at least a hundred hands high with a flat top. It appeared to be entirely surrounded by black water, like a wide moat around a castle. Before them stretched a narrow causeway of stone, obviously man-made and ancient. The causeway led across the water to the base of the hill. Zaggie said, "I suggest we leave it be and go around it."

Once again, Itus appeared beside them. "What's that big hill in front of us?"

"It's an ancient Ghoulvat burial site," answered the cat. "We must not disturb it."

Itus did not reply immediately. He glanced up past the ever-present ravens in the treetops to study the evening sky. Finally, he said to Gartho, "I suppose it's soon going to be too dark to continue our march. As much as I regret it, we'd best camp here for the night." He turned to Hoops. "Is that road leading across to the hill safe to use?"

"Looks like it is, General. Havoc and I can check it out. But don't you think it would be wise to camp here and then in the morning, just skirt around the bog, leaving that place alone?"

"I'm a soldier, Wiffin. For defensive reasons, soldiers always take the high ground when the opportunity presents itself. We're going to make camp on that hill.   Who knows whether some creatures, like a band of Skaggs, might decide to harass us during the night?"

"If that's your decision, then may I suggest you have the men gather firewood for cooking and take it across from here to the mound? There doesn't seem to be any on that treeless pile of rocks," Hoops said.

Itus grunted and strolled to the rear of the formation, while Gartho ordered his men to gather kindling. A moonless night had enveloped the mire by the time the exhausted band reached the flat summit of the burial site. Hastily, they built a circle of campfires and broke out their cooking utensils and food supplies which consisted mainly of venison jerky and salted fish. Hoops, with Zaggie beside him, was seated with several strangely silent legionnaires around one of the fires when he overheard an agitated Itus talking to Var just a few paces behind him. "I ordered you not to leave her side for an instant, Var. You're supposed to have a firm grip on her chain at all times."

"Believe me, General, she's not going to try to escape while we are still in this swamp. She knows the chances she'll end up dying in some sinkhole or a bog if she tries to run away. Like the rest of us, she's dependent on that Wiffin to guide us through this mire."

"I don't know about that, Var. You can't trust a Gretien, especially one as reckless as that girl."

Var replied, "Trust me, General. I'll make sure she's in tow on a chain as soon as we get out of here. It's just that it's rough going through this mire and having to drag her along with that chain makes it even rougher for me."

Hoops couldn't hear the rest of the conversation as the two soldiers moved away, strolling along the perimeter of the campsite. He glanced around him and finally spotted Javala. The girl was alone, except for Havoc napping beside her. She was seated on a rock before a fire at the far end of the summit.

"Var has left her alone for once," said Zaggie. "If you want to talk with her, now is your opportunity."

"What am I to say to her? She hates me for saving Itus."

"You'll think of something. It's important that she is on our side, Hoops. If we survive this night, she may prove most helpful to us later on. Now, go and talk to her!"

Hoops was about to remind Zaggie that he refused to take orders from a cat, but decided against arguing with an animal. After some hesitation, he got up and strolled over to the fire where Javala was methodically preparing a meal of salted sea mullet.

"May I join you?"

Javala glanced up. Warm, dancing patterns of orange and yellow firelight flickered over her face. But her eyes were black ice. Havoc glanced up at Hoops, wagged his tail briefly, and went back to sleep.

"Javala, please believe me. I am sorry about the incident with Itus."

"You should have let that beast die."

Hoops was thoughtful for a moment. "You consider yourself a warrior, right?"

"I am a warrior."

"Then perhaps I did you a favor. I intervened with the Goddess of Fate to save Itus from drowning. Someday, the gods willing, you might be able to face him in combat like a true warrior."

"You've done me no favor, Wiffin," she retorted. "Don't try to excuse your stupid action with an equally stupid justification." She turned her attention back to the simmering clay pot of fish.

Hoops wanted to say something more, but he didn't know what. Perhaps it was best to let Javala's temper cool on its own. Then he remembered Itus's remark after he had saved the general's life. Itus had clearly warned Hoops that both he and Javala might be killed as soon as they were no longer useful to him. Once the legionnaires were safely through the land of the Skaggs, certainly Javala no longer would be needed. "You must try to escape first thing after daylight tomorrow," Hoops said to her. "Var doesn't plan to drag you around on that chain. At least, not while we're still in the Great Mire. I overheard him arguing with Itus that you won't try to escape until we get out of here because you know you'll most likely disappear into one of those sinkholes. If you do try to get away while we're still in the Great Mire, then do it only when there's enough light to see a few paces ahead. You must watch out for little heart-shaped red mushrooms sprouting up from what looks like solid ground. Avoid the mushrooms and you avoid the invisible sinkholes. Understand?" Javala nodded, but her eyes remained dark and expressionless. Hoops wished he could fathom her thoughts.

Hoops turned to walk away when she said suddenly, "Are you one of those people who would save a drowning jackal knowing full well that the creature would sink his teeth into your hand the moment it was safe?"

"I suppose I am, Javala. That's how I got my knee injured. When I was very young, I saved a bear cub from a bog. The critter animal turned on me the moment it was on firm ground. I've been hurting off and on ever since."

"Obviously, you learned scant little from that incident."

Hoops detected a trace of warmth, perhaps even humor in that remark.

Var appeared out of the dark. "I warn you, Wiffin. You're not to be talking with this Gretien prisoner. Leave her be. I mean now!"

Hoops left them and walked over to a campfire where Captain Gartho was seated, a wooden bowl in one hand, and a long dagger in the other. He was spearing chunks of boiled meat and wolfing them down greedily.

Zaggie was beside him, nibbling on one piece he had dished out to her. From the cat's expression, Hoops knew she found the meal distasteful, but hunger overshadowed her delicate taste buds.

"You had best eat something, Wiffin, while it's still hot," the sternfaced Gartho said. "This dry, seasoned kindling is burning up too fast. I've sent a couple of soldiers back down the hill to scrounge more wood." The captain jabbed into the bowl, retrieved a portion of meat, and presented it, dangling from the point of his dagger, to

Hoops. Hoops thanked him and began chewing on the warm water-logged meat.

"Notice those wailing spirits—Ghoulvats, you call 'em?—have finally shut up. That's a good omen or bad?"

"Good. Maybe we can get some sleep tonight."

"It's bad," said Zaggie. "Remember that silence often reigns before the first peal of thunder."

"Can't say I agree with—" Hoops said, but he was cut off mid-sentence by a high-pitched scream of agony. The cry came from below, near the base of the burial mound.

Gartho was on his feet instantly, clutching his meat-laden dagger in his left hand and quickly drawing his sword with his right. "That was no spirit. That was a human's cry of pain!"

"So it seems," said Zaggie calmly. "I fear the Keepers of the Tomb, the Klackclaws, have come to punish us for trespassing on this sacred hill."

Gartho ignored Zaggie's comment. He ordered two stunned legionnaires seated nearby to grab lighted brands from the campfire and follow him down the side of the mound. Hoops was right behind them, as they stumbled and slid down the moss-coated side of the mound to the water's edge. At first, there was nothing to be seen. The two legionnaires with their makeshift torches fanned out along the base of the mound. Gartho accompanied one of them. Hoops and the other legionnaire went in the opposite direction.

"What's happened down there?" came the booming voice of Itus from above.

"We don't know yet," the captain shouted back. "We're looking."

Hoops heard Itus shouting orders to other legionnaires, and almost immediately, four more torch-bearing soldiers, including Var, joined the group at the bottom of the slope. The rocks along the water's edge were slimy and Hoops slipped, slamming his tender knee on the stones. He regained his footing only to go down again. He was on hands and knees, scrambling to get back up when, instead of a hard rock, he felt one of his palms press down on something soft and sticky. "By Zob!" he heard himself say and immediately jerked away his hand. "We need a torch over here," he yelled. Var and a legionnaire carrying a torch in one hand and a javelin in the other were beside him almost instantly.

"May the Supreme Power save us," muttered Var, as he stared down into the circle of yellow torchlight bouncing off the damp stones. On the rocks lay a blood-smeared human arm, cut off at the elbow. Lifeless fingers still clung tightly to the hilt of a legionnaire's sword. Its blade looked like a twisted piece of scrap metal.

"I demand to know what's going on down there!" Itus shouted at the stunned group.

Var glanced up at the summit and started to shout back a reply, but he never got the chance. The still black water of the bog erupted violently. Var spun around, sword overhead in a striking position, while the legionnaire swung his torch in the direction of the bog. In the dancing torchlight, Hoops caught a glimpse of a gigantic scorpionlike creature rearing up over them from the water, monstrous pincers snapping viciously like the clashing of steel blades. With a loud hiss, the creature stretched out a claw toward Var.

Var, holding his sword in both hands, slashed at it with all his strength. With a sharp metallic clang, the weapon bounced harmlessly off the creature's black scales. Var raised his sword and swung again. This time, the impact of the blow knocked the weapon from Var's grasp and sent it flying into the bog. A desperate, defenseless Var turned his back and started to scramble back up the mound, but the creature was quicker. It lashed out again with a claw and caught the Var by the neck. A torrent of warm blood sprayed Hoops. He heard a sickening thud. He looked down to see Var's severed head, eyes bulging, rolling to a stop on the rocks by his feet.

The legionnaire at Hoops's side shouted a Sarien battle cry and hurled his iron-tipped javelin at the creature looming over them. With a clang, the javelin bounced off the creature's scaly body into the water. The monster opened its reptilian jaws, hissed violently, and lunged forward. The legionnaire then flung his torch at the creature's head. The flaming brand struck the creature between its bulbous green eyes. It screamed and backed away from the slope to slip beneath the surface of the bog, taking Var's headless body with it.

For a moment, there was utter silence, save for the heavy breathing of Hoops and the legionnaire. But the stillness was shattered by the shouts of alarm from the small group of legionnaires accompanying Gartho. The shouts were followed by the clash of swords against scales, as two more creatures emerged from the bog to advance on the soldiers.

"Swords are useless against them," Hoops shouted to Captain Gartho. "They seem to be afraid of fire. Use your torches to keep them at bay!" Hoops turned to his legionnaire companion. "Let's get back up the hill near the campfires. We'll need more torches." Without waiting for a reply, Hoops began scrambling up the rocks. The legionnaire, uttering an obscenity at every step, followed on his heels. Gasping for breath, his knee throbbing, Hoops reached the flat summit of the burial mound only to find Gartho and his men already there, poking sticks of firewood into the campfires to make additional torches.

Itus shouted orders to the men. "Gather the horses inside the ring of campfires. Then form up in a defensive formation around the perimeter. The winged cat says these creatures are Klackclaws. Their scales are too tough for our weapons, but they are backing away from fire. I want every legionnaire armed with a torch in each hand. Forget drawn swords."

Itus called for Hoops. When Hoops reached his side, the general lowered his voice and said, "I need you to do some fast scouting. The men report that these Klackclaws have gathered at the base of this cursed mound. But so far, only in front of us and only at the bottom of the slope we climbed to get up here. None of the troops have spotted any Klackclaws around the backside of this hill of rocks." He paused briefly and looked around, studying the circle of firelight. "In case you haven't noticed, we didn't lug much firewood up here. What wood we have is very dry and burns quickly. It won't be long before we'll run out. Once that happens or so your strange cat advises me, the Klackclaws will crawl up the slope and overrun us. She's probably right. So I'm ordering you, little Wiffin, to find another causeway or strip of dry land or whatever on the backside of this hill so I can get my men out of this trap. Understand?"

"I understand," Hoops muttered nervously.

"Then, get moving! Any moment, those monsters might decide to circle the entire mound and cut us off from any hope of retreat."

Hoops started to limp away, but Itus reached out his iron claw and stopped him. "One other thing, Hoops," snarled the general. "If you fail to find us a way out of here, forget about crawling back. If the Klackclaws don't end your miserable life, rest assured that I will do the job. Now be off!"

Chapter 12

Hoops and Havoc inched their way in total darkness down the steep slope until they reached the bog at the foot of the north side of the mound. There they paused, listening for any sound indicating Klackclaws were lurking nearby. The only sound that reached them was the sudden clamoring of legionnaires on the summit above. One of the Klackclaws on the other side of the mound must have gotten too close to the top, Hoops thought. He listened for an agonized scream from a soldier or maybe from Javala. He has last seen her standing, torch in hand, side by side with the legionnaires.

There were no screams. Silence returned. The legionnaires must have succeeded in frightening off the creature with their torches. "Thank you, Zob," he said under his breath. Hoops couldn't immediately decide to turn left or right along the base of the burial ground. He felt certain that the ancient Ghoulvats or whoever had built the tomb and the causeway leading to it from one side most likely had constructed another causeway across the bog to the opposite side.

During a visit to his grandfather's cavern, he noticed some sketches of ancient burial grounds compiled by a Wiffin historian. All the tomb sites appeared to have designed with two approach routes. When Hoops had asked about this, the old wizard replied that one route was for transporting the body to the tomb. The other road was for the spirit to use when leaving the gravesite to go to the heavens or to hell.

Hoops was about to turn right when a momentary break in the low clouds allowed a glimmer of moonlight to filter through to the

Great Mire. To his left, Hoops spotted what appeared to be another causeway stretching out across the bog. He was about to scramble back up the mound to immediately report his discovery to Itus but changed his mind. Perhaps, he'd best do a little more exploring to make certain this was indeed a manmade causeway, or at least a finger of high ground crossing the entire width of the bog. The light was dim, and from where he and Havoc stood, he couldn't be sure. He didn't want to lead the band along with horses into an even worse trap, a dead end in the middle of a Klackclaw-infested bog.

Hoops and Havoc continued to silently edge the base of the mound until they reached the causeway. As Hoops had prayed, it was indeed a man created road of stone, now well covered with moss and a crust of long dead vegetation. Hoops, with Havoc in the lead, followed it out about halfway across to the other side. Satisfied that the causeway did span the entire moat-like bog, he began retracing his steps to report his findings to Itus. "We'd best hurry," he said aloud to Havoc. "It looks like the fires on the summit are getting dimmer. They must be running really low on wood." Havoc snorted a reply and started to loop back along the causeway toward the hill of rocks.

The wolf suddenly stopped. His head was up, sniffing the air. "What is it?" Hoops asked.

The question was answered an explosion of water nearby. Two Klackclaws broke through the surface of the water and began grinding their way up the side of the burial site toward the besieged legionnaires. A third monster emerged from the bog where the causeway connected with the burial ground. Despite the poor lighting, Hoops realized that this creature was not looking up at the mound.

It was looking directly down the causeway to where Hoops and Havoc stood riveted. Hoops tried not to move a muscle, but his whole body was trembling. Had the creature seen him? The Klackclaw remained motionless, like a viper coiled and ready to strike once it determined the precise location of its prey. A frightened Havoc made the first move. With tail between his legs, the wolf noisily darted off along the causeway. The Klackclaw reared up and, with pincers snapping violently, launched itself forward in Hoops's direction.

Hoops heard himself cry out in fright as he turned and raced along the stone causeway following Havoc. He reached the far side of the bog and plunged into the dead forest. There was no going back now. The legionnaires, Javala, and Zaggie were totally surrounded. They were doomed once the fires burn out. Hoops felt an overwhelming nausea. He paused for an instant and, bracing himself against a tree trunk, vomited violently. He jerked when something brushed against his knee, but it was only Havoc who had returned to check on him.

"I'm all right. Let's get moving," he told the wolf. Once again, he scrambled through the dead forest, heedless of the noise he was making. But he didn't get far. He tripped over a fallen log and toppled forward, his head jarring against something unyielding. An angry white flash shot across his eyes. He felt himself fading into total darkness, but he struggled against it.

He finally reopened his eyes, wondering if he had fallen unconscious, and if so, for how long? His head, like his knee, was throbbing. He was lying on his side at the base of a tree. He felt blood oozing down his cheek.

"Aye, Wiffin, seems you banged yourself up good, slamming your head into an ancient tree like you just did."

Hoops jerked into a sitting position and looked around him. He spied Havoc nearby. The wolf was cleaning his front feet, apparently unaware of anyone else.

"Who's that?" Hoops asked the darkness. Maybe he was hearing voices. A blow to the head could do funny things to the mind.

"Just me, your old friend, the hunter. You remember, don't you? We crossed paths back at the hamlet."

"Where are you? I don't see anyone." But Hoops recognized the almost whimsical voice.

"I'm just around." The voice came from a different direction now as if the hunter was silently circling Hoops. But none of the surrounding shadows were moving.

"What are you doing here, hunter?"

"I'm hunting, of course. But you're running," came the reply.

"I have no choice. The wolf and I are the only ones to escape the Klackclaws."

"Where are you running to?" asked the hunter. This question, almost a whisper, came from behind Hoops.

"If you must know, hunter, I'm on a mission to try to save my homeland. Nothing must stop me." Hoops felt anger swelling up. "Why all the questions? Why do you care what I'm doing?"

The hunter was silent for a moment, then he said quietly, "You must have dug deep into your soul to answer the question of what comes first: saving your friends or saving your homeland. A decision like that is always a wee bit difficult to make, is it not? Naturally, you can't let fear enter into that kind of decision-making. But, of course, Wiffin, you know that. Guess it isn't pleasant being in your boots right now. Glad I'm not."

"Damn you, hunter!" Hoops felt the veins on his neck growing tight. "How dare you call me a coward. You're afraid to even show yourself to me. I call that cowardly."

The hunter chuckled softly. "I don't recall calling you a coward. But I must say you're taking offense too easily. Could it be you have some lingering doubts deep within you about the decision you've made, putting your mission ahead of your friends including that rather charming Gretien girl and your most unusual cat?"

"Doubts play no role in this, hunter!" Hoops was shouting now, heedless of whether Klackclaws lurking nearby might hear him. "There is no way I can help those souls atop the burial mound. When the fires are extinguished, so will be their lives."

"Aye, indeed the Klackclaws are afraid of flames. Just imagine, Wiffin, how those creatures must envision hell. Perhaps to find themselves encircled by a blazing forest? Bet that would scare 'em right out of their scales." The hunter chuckled.

"Oh well, Wiffin, I have hunting to do and you have your mission. So, I bid you farewell and good luck in your venture."

Hoops jumped to his feet. "Show yourself before you leave, hunter!" But the unseen hunter was gone. Had he ever really been there? Hoops's mind was blurred. He felt dizzy. He sat back down on the forest floor, his back against a tree, massaging his knee. Havoc nuzzled him and began to lick the blood from his head wound. Hoops tried to gather his thoughts. He still had a long journey ahead to Dourghoul Keep. The weather was going to worsen this time of year. He already felt chilled. He had left his cloak atop the mound, along with his leather satchel of dried meat, copper meal bowl, water jug, and other limited camping equipment. The only items he had now were his knives, his belt ax, and the leather pouch dangling from his belt. The pouch only contained a few coins, his flint and steel, and his tinderbox. The tinderbox! What had the hunter said? A circle of fire? Hoops leaped to his feet. Pain stabbed at his knee, but he ignored it.

He found a dead branch about five hands long and hurriedly applied flint and steel to tinder, praying the mixture of dried moss and sulfur would ignite quickly. It did. One end of the branch caught fire almost instantly. He ordered Havoc to lead. Holding the torch out before him like a spear, Hoops began racing back the way he had come through the mire—toward the mound and the Klackclaws. He emerged from the woods and paused at the beginning of the causeway. The fires on the summit of the burial mound on the far side of the bog were much dimmer now. The night echoed with the clamorous uproar of the legionnaires trying to drive back the Klackclaws. The creatures were growing braver as the flames died down. Hoops could see them high on the slopes, closing in on the defenders. The constant snapping of their giant pincers resounded over the bog.

Hoops turned to his right, leaving the causeway, and raced along the edge of the bog for twenty or more paces before he set his first fire. He had to leave open the escape route from the burial mound. He jabbed his torch into a pile of twigs and small branches at the base of a massive tree. The debris quickly ignited. Flames shot up, feeding greedily on the dry, flaking bark of the trunk. Hoops moved as fast as he could, confident that keen-nosed Havoc would steer him clear of any mushroom-encircled sinkhole. Each time Hoops came upon a pile of forest trash along the edge of the bog, he thrust his torch into it, waited a few seconds to make certain it caught fire, and raced on.

Sweat streamed down his face, and he was struggling for breath by the time he had completed a half-circle around the bog. He reached the causeway on the other side of the mound. He paused for a few seconds, pondering whether to set a fire close by. That would block off the only other possible escape route from the burial site.

A Klackclaw shot up from the placid surface of the bog only a few yards away and hurled itself across the causeway, driving its huge armored body on stubby legs across the rocks straight at Hoops. Hoops leaped back, keeping the torch well out in front, hoping to keep the creature at bay until he could start another fire along the tree line. The Klackclaw kept advancing. Its maniacal eyes glistened red in the torchlight. Hoops stepped back once more and felt a crush of twigs beneath his heels. Without taking his eyes off the Klackclaw, he lowered his torch to the forest bed and prayed to Zob.

Flames shot up around his feet, and Hoops had to jump to one side to escape them. The Klackclaw opened its jaws, flashing long, serpentlike fangs and screamed in rage. At first, it would not retreat. But as the flames began dancing higher across the dry forest floor, the creature screamed again and slid backward into the bog and disappeared.

Hoops immediately continued his run around the perimeter of the bog, setting fires every few yards. Screams and hisses of fury from the Klackclaws and the crackling of trees aflame filled the night air. A glance back over his shoulder revealed an almost solid wall of fire roaring along the edge of the bog. Tongues of flame licked up the tall skeletal trees, sending sparks high into darkness.

In the crimson and yellow light, Hoops saw the Klackclaws sliding back down the slopes of the tomb. Water surged everywhere. The creatures were returning to the depths of the black morass. Hoops finally completed his circle and found the road he used to escape from the mound. Flames were roaring nearby and smoke clogged the air, but the causeway was still open. Waving his torch before him and shouting for all he was worth, Hoops, with Havoc at his side, raced across the bog and dashed up the side of the mound. There were no Klackclaws on the slope to greet him. None on the summit. He stumbled into a cheering crowd of legionnaires and a grinning Javala. Exhausted, he collapsed to the ground.

"Don't just lay around, Hoops," shouted a stone-faced Itus. "No time for celebrating, you fools," he screamed at his men. "Just grab your weapons and get those skittish horses moving. Leave everything else behind. We're traveling light. We've got to break out of this ring of fire before we no longer have an escape route and we all suffocate. You lead the way, Wiffin. Gartho and I will bring up the rear along with the horses and the prisoner. Move out smartly!"

Before Hoops started down the slope once again, he shouted to Javala, "Better bring your cloak. And please bring mine, if you can find it."

"Can't. We all burned our cloaks, including yours. Anything to keep the fires alive."

"Stop dawdling, Hoops!" Itus screamed. The stunned general stood motionless for a few seconds, his face drawn and pale in the crimson light of the fire roaring about him. Then he, Havoc, Hoops, and the bulk of the legionnaires rapidly found the causeway at the base of the slope and, in single file, raced across it. The forest fire closed on the roadway from both directions. The heat and blinding smoke were intense. He heard yells and curses at the rear of the column as some of the men, including Gartho and Itus, struggled to drag or push the panicked horses across the stone pathway through the bog. Hoops stopped leading the men once they had reached the end of the causeway and reentered the mire. He told the men directly behind him to keep moving, following the wolf as closely as possible. Hoops was worried that Javala and Gartho, as well, might not make it across the bog before the fires closed off the causeway. The horses, including both Itus's and the captain's, were balking at every step as sparks flew by them.

At last, they made it. Or almost. Itus's powerful steed was the last in the column. It was within a yard of shoreline when a towering, burning tree broke off at the base and slammed into the bog, throwing up steam and a shower of sparks. A blazing brand struck the horse behind its ears. The animal reared up, jerked its reins from the general's grasp, and bolted into the bog. The stunned general stood motionless for a few seconds, his face drawn and pale in the crimson light of the fire roaring about him. Then he stepped to the water's edge and appeared about to dive in to save the animal. Gartho grabbed him from behind. Itus struggled to shake off the captain who kept shouting, "Forget the horse, General. You can't drag him out of that morass. You'll only be dragged down to your death in that slime or a Klackclaw, lurking beneath the surface, will have you."

"That's my horse, Gartho. He's fought more battles with me than you ever will. I love that horse more than anything else. I'll not have him die like this."

"You have a queen's mission to perform and men to lead out of here. I won't let you do this."

"Let go of me, Gartho!" the general screamed and raised his clawed hand to strike the captain. But he didn't follow through. He suddenly stopped struggling in the captain's grasp. He lowered his head. Hoops could hear him sobbing.

The stallion was sinking fast in the bog, straining its neck to keep its head above the water. But Hoops knew it was doomed. "We have got to get out of here," he yelled at the two officers. "The fire is closing in fast about us."

"I'll save the animal," Javala said calmly, as she stepped toward the edge of the bog.

"No! You'll not try anything so stupid," growled Gartho. "Get moving." He savagely pushed her ahead of him. Then, almost gently, the captain took Itus by the elbow and escorted the general through the narrowing gap in the flames into the blackness of the Great Mire.

Hoops raced to the front of the column to take up his usual position as point man. Throughout the night without a stop, the band marched north toward the land of the fearsome Skaggs.

Chapter 13

An angry roar from Itus wrenched Hoops out of a fitful sleep. "The wretched little Gretien has escaped!" Hoops leaped to his feet and glanced about him. In the faint gray light of an overcast dawn, he could see the shadowy forms of the legionnaires, most of them still sprawled on the ground where they had collapsed, exhausted, the moment they had emerged from the Great Mire. No sign of Javala.

"She must have escaped back in the mire," mumbled a groggy Gartho. "There was a lot of confusion during our march last night. It would have been easy for her to slip away unnoticed in the dark."

"Detail some men to retrace our steps and run her down," Itus bellowed at the captain. "As much as I'd like to slit her throat right now, we still might need her. We're entering Skagmoor, and I intend to use her as a hostage if we encounter this moor's miserable little inhabitants. Do I make myself clear, Captain?"

"She could have given us the slip anywhere back in the mire, General. Unfortunately, Var was no longer around to keep an eye on her. I was too busy trying to keep the men and horses in some semblance of formation in the dark. It might take us days to track her down. By my count, we already lost two legionnaires and Var. We might lose more men looking for her. Chances are, she is dead by now. She either wandered into quicksand in the dark or those Klackclaws caught up with her."

Itus, still red-faced with rage, did not respond immediately. He paced among the men, violently slamming his good fist into his iron claw. The knuckles on his hand started bleeding. He stopped abruptly and drew several deep breaths to regain his composure. "As much as I hate to admit it, Captain, you're probably right. We can't afford to waste more time. I hope she died the slow, agonizing death that all Gretiens deserve. Get these lazy legionnaires up and moving. We've got a lot of territory yet to cover. Tell your men to pray we don't run into a large force of Skaggs or we all will be as dead as my beloved horse and that cursed girl."

The men were slow getting to their feet. Hoops had lost track of time, but he guessed the group had gotten no more than an hour's sleep at most. They no longer had their cloaks or blankets and, even in the faint light, he could see that most of the men, clad only in short, sleeveless crimson tunics and light armor, were visibly shivering from the damp chill that hung over Skagmoor. Although he was wearing his leather jerkin and leggings, Hoops felt the cold stealing into his body. His knee stiffened.

Zaggie appeared at Hoops's feet. "I saw Javala slip away in the night. She did it very soon after we had crossed over the bog where Itus's horse was floundering in the ooze."

"I warned her not to try to escape until daylight so she could spot the dry sinkholes in the Great Mire," returned Hoops. "Why she didn't listen to my advice is beyond me."

Zaggie replied, "Perhaps she felt she had no choice but to attempt to get away when chaos reigned among the soldiers. After all, it's daylight now and it would be too late for her to attempt an escape under the watchful eyes of Itus and his men. Javala took her chances. I'll credit her for sheer audacity."

"I really liked Javala, although the gods know I was afraid of her at times. It's a horrible shame. I blame myself for her death. I was the one who advised her to escape when she got the chance. Her death is on my head, Zaggie."

"Don't blame yourself, my dear Hoops. I believe you gave her the best advice you could under the circumstances. You can't always hold yourself accountable for other people's actions.

"I knew from the moment we met her, she was going to cause us trouble. She did. But believe it or not, I, too, sorely will miss her and so will your wolf companion."

Hoops glanced at Havoc. The wolf's pale blue eyes were dull and lifeless, staring back at the mist-shrouded Great Mire. "Let's get going, Havoc. Grieving will not help us now. We may have the Skaggs to contend with. I'm again trusting your keen sense of smell to give us first warning if they appear." Havoc flicked his ear to register he understood Hoops. Slowly, the wolf fell into formation for the march across Skagmoor.

Monochrome swirls of threatening rain clouds hung low over the expanse of low, winter-dead grass, punctuated by splotches of gray-green bracken and lichen-coated outcrops of stark granite. Havoc had moved out ahead of the column, nose in the air, sniffing the moisture-laden breeze that swept across the moor from the west. Hoops and Captain Gartho, who, as usual, was walking alongside his mount carrying Zaggie, led the troops. "The Skaggs generally prefer to hunt in the western part of Skagmoor. More game over there. We may well make it to Dourghoul Keep without incident if we stay to the east," Zaggie volunteered.

"As usual, you seemed very well-informed," said Gartho. "Frankly, I've never encountered any Skaggs. I hear the little creatures rely entirely on poison darts and blowguns. Is that right, Zaggie?"

"Indeed. And they won't do battle unless they well outnumber us. Then they simply will surround us and, from a safe distance, rain down hundreds of poison darts until we are all dead. Your legionnaires might kill a few of them with arrows, but they are tiny animals and very difficult to hit."

"Any more advice, Zaggie?" said Hoops.

"No. But I must say, I'm surprised that your legionnaires didn't bring along shields on this mission. Shields might have helped defend against some of the darts. Although, if it came to a major confrontation, I fear we'd be killed no matter what."

"General Itus said nothing to me about going into Skagg territory," Gartho said to the cat in a sharp, defensive tone. "Had I known we'd be marching across Skagmoor, you can be assured I'd have ordered my men to carry shields, as much as we of the Fourth Legion detest taking them into battle against ordinary soldiers."

"It would seem that your great Lord General Itus is to blame for the oversight," murmured Zaggie.

Hoops noticed for the first time that none of the legionnaires were carrying their trusted javelins or lances. The soldiers must have resorted to using their weapons' wooden shafts as torches in the struggle against the Klackclaws. Except for a few archers, the rest of the troops were armed only with swords. A wolf's howl erupted from an outcrop of rock about a furlong ahead of the column.

"It's Havoc," said Hoops. "He's obviously sensed danger."

"I saw two gophers yonder, Captain," reported a nearby legionnaire. The soldier was pointing to a jagged mound of large granite slabs about a hundred yards to their right. "They were atop those rocks. Maybe that wolf is just getting hungry and smells a good meal around here." He chuckled. "Reckon, we could all use some fresh meat. Want me to wander over there and see if I can kill one or more for a noontime meal?"

"Absolutely not," replied Gartho. "We are here to march, not hunt. Besides," the captain noted. "The general isn't about to grant us a break before we get across Skagmoor. Mark my words."

"Smoke from cooking fires might be spotted from some distance away by Skagg scouts. We don't need to draw attention to ourselves," added Hoops.

Havoc howled again. The wolf was out of sight, over a low rise in the otherwise flat landscape. "He's not hunting," muttered Hoops. "Wolves are silent when stalking prey. He's warning us."

"Look over to our left," said Zaggie from atop Gartho's tall horse. "From up here, I see four more gopherlike creatures standing upright in the grass. Only, I'm afraid they are not gophers."

"What are they, Zaggie?" asked Hoops. He was standing on his tiptoes but couldn't see anything moving in the grass.

"I see them," said the much taller Gartho. "They don't look like rabbits or hares. Ears are too short."

"I'm afraid they're Skaggs," replied the cat. "Now, look to our right. There must be three score or more emerging from behind that mound of granite. I don't like the looks of this. Perhaps we should suggest to the lord general that we retreat back into the Great Mire while we still can."

Gartho turned to one of his legionnaires and was about to order him to summon Itus from the rear of the column when suddenly the general appeared beside them. His face was taut, emphasizing the webwork of battle scars fanning across it.

"Damn Skaggs are showing up by the droves behind us," he told Gartho. "We're cut off from the mire. Get the men up to the top of that low ridge in front of us and order them to take up defensive positions. I want the men—"

Zaggie interrupted him. "Too late, General!"

They all glanced at the top of the ridge. A diminutive but formidable wall of tiny creatures had appeared on the high ground in front of the band. The brown fur-covered Skaggs, each armed with a blowgun, stood motionless, obviously waiting for further orders. But where was Havoc? Hoops felt a sickening feeling invade his whole body. The last they had heard from Havoc was his howl of warning and that had come from the far side of the ridge. "Please, Zob. First, Javala, and now, Havoc? Are Zaggie and I next? Why are you abandoning us?"

A legionnaire raced up from the rear of the formation, shouting, "General, a rider is approaching us from the direction of the Great Mire. The horse is enormous. I swear it looks like your stallion."

Keen-eyed Zaggie spun around on her saddle and looked back. "Indeed, Lord General, that's your mount. And judging from the flaming red hair and that dirty, sleeveless jacket, that's Javala astride it."

"Impossible," muttered a stunned Itus.

Zaggie ignored the general's remark. "I can make out a band of Skaggs hopping along in the grass around her like an escort. She's not heading for us. She appears to be on a parallel course."

Itus peered off into the gray distance and shook his head in disbelief. "My horse has never allowed anyone except me to ride him, let alone a filthy Gretien prisoner. I can't believe this is happening."

"That girl has a way with animals," said Hoops.

"I beg your pardon, Hoops, but she certainly didn't impress me at first," retorted Zaggie.

Gartho was the first to spot a roe buck carrying a small creature on its back, approaching across the moor from the west. The deer and rider were headed straight for Javala. A white falcon was circling above.

"That must be Yukman, the elderly chief of the Skaggs. I recognize his falcon," Zaggie told the group.

Hoops glanced up at Zaggie and asked sharply, "What do you mean, *I recognize Yukman's falcon?*"

Zaggie didn't answer the question. "Unless I'm mistaken, which I rarely am, that's Havoc loping through the bracken toward Javala and Yukman."

"Thank you, Zob," a relieved Hoops mumbled under his breath the moment he also spotted the wolf making its way between clusters of Skaggs grouped like bodyguards around both Javala and their chieftain. Hoops was amazed. The tiny Skaggs seemed unconcerned about a giant wolf in their midst.

The band of soldiers watched in uneasy silence, as Javala reined in the horse and dismounted to greet Yukman. The Skagg leader remained straddled on the back of his mount while the two talked. Periodically, Javala could be seen gesturing in the direction of the legionnaires.

"She is most likely asking Yukman to kill us all," growled Itus. Without warning, the general grabbed Hoops by the neck, drew his sword, and pressed its point just beneath the Wiffin's ear. "You are going to substitute as hostage, Hoops. I trust she can see you and me from where she's standing. And, for your sake, I hope she's not so willing to watch you die by my hand."

"I fear that putting your sword to this Wiffin's throat will only serve to infuriate her more," Gartho said angrily. "I suggest you lower your blade, and let's wait to see what the Skaggs intend to do. They don't seem ready to attack us. At least, not for the moment."

"I'll decide how to handle a hostage situation, Captain." The general pressed the sword harder against Hoops's flesh. Hoops felt a trickle of blood on his neck. Silence settled over the troops while they watched Javala and Yukman converse. Finally, Javala gave the minuscule Skagg leader a hug and returned to Itus's horse. A few seconds later, she was riding toward the band of men. The white falcon hovered above her.

"What's her game?" Itus wondered aloud. "She's coming right at us."

Javala dismounted gracefully a short distance from the legionnaires and led the general's horse over to him. She handed the reins to Itus. "A splendid animal," she said calmly. "Much too fine for the likes of you, Itus."

"Watch your tongue, girl!" snapped the general. Itus lowered the sword, although he kept Hoops collared in a powerful grip.

"Please explain what is going on, Javala?" said Gartho. "I'm totally confused. Why did you return to us? You could have escaped on horseback to your own lands and left our fate in the hands of the Skaggs."

"Suffice it to say, Captain, you and your men have Yukman's personal word that you can continue on to Dourghoul Keep," replied Javala. Her voice was cold. "But there are certain conditions."

"I won't tolerate having conditions imposed on me from some furry little creature I could crush to death in the palm of one hand," Itus hissed. The general's grip on Hoops's neck drew even tighter.

"What are the conditions?" a choking Hoops managed to blurt out.

Javala glanced up at the sky. The white falcon was making lazy circles above her. "See that bird? He is going to keep watch over us for the rest of our journey. If any of you threaten me or Hoops or try to fetter us with ropes or chains, that falcon will report your actions to Yukman. Yukman swears that he and his Skaggs will immediately track you down and kill you all. In fact, Yukman told me to tell you, Lord General Itus, that he will personally kill you with a dart coated with the most painful and slow-acting poison the Skaggs have developed. Trust me, Itus, the Skaggs are geniuses when it comes to concocting poisons. By the way, General, I suggest you let go of Hoops. The falcon might misinterpret what is going at this very moment. In that case, I doubt you and your men will ever make it alive over the next ridge." Itus hesitated for several seconds. Then, he abruptly exhaled and let go of Hoops.

"Thank the gods," mumbled a relieved Gartho.

"Hoops and I are going to have a private conversation, Itus. I trust you will have enough sense not to interfere," Javala said. She motioned for Hoops to follow her. When they were out of hearing distance from the band of confused and apprehensive legionnaires, they halted.

"What's this all about, Javala? Why did you return only to become a prisoner again?"

"Because I swore to Yukman that I will do everything possible to help you and Zaggie accomplish your mission."

"What are you saying? You don't know anything about our mission. Don't tell me that Yukman knows all about it. Impossible!"

"I grant you it is all very strange to me, especially since I have no idea why we're going to Dourghoul Keep. I only know that's our destination because I overheard the soldiers grumbling about it. After Yukman and I exchanged greetings, he informed me that my brother was alive. Then—"

Hoops interrupted. "By Zob, that's great news!"

Javala nodded, but she didn't smile. "Yukman also gave me some news about my clan that was most discouraging. But I'll tell you about that later. The Skagg chieftain cheerfully announced that he was going to kill all the legionnaires. He really relished the idea. There was thick drool dribbling from his fangs when he spoke. That's always a sign that a Skagg is happy and excited. I told him you were among that bunch." She glanced back at the legionnaires huddled around their officers. "And if they showered down their darts, you'd probably die like the rest. He replied that he expected you would die, but that the life of a single Wiffin meant little to the Skaggs. He was determined to kill Itus.

"Then his little eyes fastened upon Zaggie sitting on Gartho's horse. Skaggs have remarkable vision. He asked about the cat. I told him the cat belonged to you. Unexpectedly, he asked me if the cat had wings? I nodded and immediately, Yukman's whole demeanor changed. He got very pensive. Finally, he exclaimed, 'We cannot allow anything to happen to Zaggie. She must be on a mission of the utmost importance.' He made me swear that I would accompany you and Zaggie until your mission is completed. I must assist both of you in every way possible. I was reluctant to agree at first. My clansmen may be in trouble and I want to rejoin them as quickly as possible. But Yukman remained adamant. Finally, I gave in to him and swore I'd help you and Zaggie the best I could.

"Yukman looked very relieved." Javala continued. "But then he saw Itus put a sword to your throat, and his beady eyes turned red with anger. For an instant, I was afraid he might lose his temper and order his Skaggs to attack immediately, no matter what. Thankfully, he didn't. Instead, he calmed down and told me what to tell Itus. He ordered his falcon to escort us until we are within sight of Dourghoul Keep. Then the bird is to return to him. He's fearful of allowing his prize falcon too near the home of the great witch."

"Did he say why he's fearful?" Hoops asked.

"No. We hugged, and he sent me on my way back to you. And that's as much as I can report, Hoops."

"Did you tell Yukman that the cat was named Zaggie?"

Javala shook her head. "But as soon as I said the cat had strange wings, he uttered her name."

Perplexed, Hoops glanced over at Zaggie who seemed to be cat-napping contentedly atop Gartho's horse. "I know better than to ask that tight-lipped creature for an explanation. I guess we'll have to wait until we get to Dourghoul Keep to find out what's really going on."

Chapter 14

"It's the most foreboding place I've ever laid eyes on," Javala whispered. "I'd feel more comfortable if Yukman's little falcon was still hovering above us."

She, Hoops, Zaggie, and Havoc stood midway across an ancient, rickety drawbridge spanning the dank moat around Dourghoul Keep. A fine, cold drizzle misted the night air. The ominous tower of vine-snarled black stone loomed over them. A rumble of distant thunder rolled across the moor.

"No sign of light inside the castle," Hoops noted. "Looks deserted. Maybe the witch is already dead." From deep within the massive fortress came the muffled howl of a wolf. Havoc snarled. His hackles bristled.

"She's alive," said Zaggie confidently. "We'd best not tarry any longer. Don't forget that Itus swore he'd storm the keep and come looking for us if we're not back out with the talisman at the crack of dawn. That doesn't give us much time."

The massive doors of the castle creaked open as the four approached. They stepped into a vast entrance hall of damp, moss-coated stone. A sphere of dull green light floated overhead, revealing two broad stairways ascending into total darkness on either side of the hall. "We'll take the left stairway," said Zaggie.

"How do you know which stairway to take?" Hoops demanded.

Zaggie replied irritably, "You've been asking me silly questions ever since we left the Skaggs. Have faith, Hoops. I know what I'm doing."

They climbed the stairs. The green light drifted lazily in front of them. They reached a landing where two black wolves with hostile crimson eyes stood guard. Havoc slunk back behind Hoops who reached for his belt ax. "No need to get alarmed," Zaggie said calmly. "I'll handle them." The cat walked over to one of the wolves and rubbed against its front legs. The wolf sniffed Zaggie, whimpered like a puppy, went down on all fours, and promptly rolled over on its back in total submission. The second wolf did the same. Hoops and Javala carefully stepped around the prostrate wolves. Havoc hesitated, then followed. A few paces further and they found themselves before a tall oaken door covered with carvings of grotesque, deformed beasts.

One of the carvings immediately caught Hoops's attention. It was a cat with batlike wings. The door swung open. "Welcome home, my dear sister! Please do come in and introduce me to your companions." The voice from within was a woman's but tinged with a brutish, rasping undertone.

Peals of angry thunder erupted outside the castle walls as the group stepped across the threshold into the chambers of the great sorceress, Tajine. Candles and wrought iron braziers of glowing coals painted the immense room with a dancing display of iridescent light. Opulent tapestries of silk interwoven with gold and silver threads adorned the walls. Intricately carved furnishings were strewn with manuscripts and ancient scrolls. Statues of demonic bestial beings in gold and bronze crowded the room. Thick furs carpeted the floor. A fire crackled on a stone hearth in one corner. In another corner where the light was much dimmer stood an enormous canopied bed surrounded by silent but alert wolves. Someone—or something—lay on the bed, body covered by layers of lavishly decorated blankets. Its features were hidden beneath a bloodflecked white veil. Beside the bed lay the bloody, partially eaten carcass of a goat.

"I must say, Zaggie, you haven't aged at all in these many decades since we parted," said the figure on the bed. "Perhaps I did you a favor when I transformed you into a cat. Unfortunately, I had no intention of bestowing on you those silly, useless wings. Forgive me for my mistake, dear sister. I'm afraid that my powers were not very refined back then."

Zaggie leaped onto the foot of the bed. "On the other hand, you, Tajine, seemed to have changed dramatically over the decades. I have the impression your powers are not all that refined, even now."

"True. As much as I've tried, I have never mastered the art of being able to undo what changes I've made to other beings, including you or to myself." The witch pulled both arms from under the blankets, exposing her hands. One was a slender, beautifully chiseled hand of a woman, the other, a furry, blunt wolf's paw. "Do not ask to see my face, Zaggie. The apparition might frighten Armarugh's grandson or this young Gretien you've brought along to my—our—Doughoul Keep." She paused. "But, please, forgive me for not asking earlier the name of this young lady?"

"I'm named Javala."

"So you are the famed warrior princess, daughter of Javalius. I understand you even make the fearless General Itus a shade nervous. That's simply marvelous! I'm honored to have you as a guest, be it even for too short a time."

"You must know that a convoy of Sarien legionnaires are stationed at the other end of the drawbridge, waiting for Hoops to exit with the talisman," said Zaggie pointedly. "They intend to make certain the talisman is delivered to Queen Saragata."

"Of course, I know about the legionnaires. My wolves warned me they were coming. I understand Itus himself is with them. I only regret my powers have faded away almost entirely as the result of my self-inflicted illness. Otherwise, I might have changed the lord general into a toad. Or perhaps a timid, toothless field mouse? Ah yes, the mouse image might have better suited the haughty general." She chuckled. To Hoops, it sounded more like a throaty growl.

The witch's tone turned serious. "As for Queen Saragata, she is a well-meaning ruler. I admire the way she has held together her diverse empire, although real credit for this achievement should go to Sar's perpetual enemy, the Lughs. On the other hand, if it wasn't for the Lughs, I expect the queen would have dismissed that silly God of War, Brutius, a long time ago. She has allowed that conceited, party-going fraud of a deity to have too much say in how she runs her kingdom. It's a true pity. I imagine Brutius figures somehow into Saragata's demands that I turn the talisman over to her. She won't have it and for good reasons."

Hoops and Javala stood with their backs to the fireplace, trying to get warm. Havoc lay curled at their feet. He eyed suspiciously the circle of silent wolves around Tajine. The witch turned her attention to Hoops. "So, you're the one Armarugh entrusted with spiriting the talisman to Wiffin land? I'm surprised at his choice. He had assured me that you could get in and out of Sar without detection. Seems he was wrong."

"It was my fault that Hoops ran into problems," interjected Javala.

"No matter whose fault it is, Javala, the fact remains that you will have to depart by the secret passage under the moat on the back side of this fortress to avoid Itus and his minions. Zaggie should be able to show you the way to the tunnel. After all, as children, we used to play *tag the dragon* in that tunnel, didn't we, Zaggie?"

"Yes. And as I recall, you usually won at that game."

"True. Many times, I have regretted that we could not return to those carefree days. Be truthful with me, dear sister. Will you continue on with the work, the experiments that our mother began and I've continued? Or when I'm dead and you're the mistress of Dourghoul Keep, will you turn back from that path into the unknown and only follow the path of the White Arts? I recall that, as a child, you were always trying to heal injured little animals with your fledgling magical powers."

"I'll stay the path of the White Arts," replied Zaggie somberly. "To cure a creature, beast or human, is one thing. But to transform that creature into an entirely different being, a being that the Supreme Power never intended to exist, that is a sacrilege. I would have thought you'd have learned your lesson by now, Tajine. Our mother died because of her unholy experiments. And shortly, you'll be dead, dear sister, for the same reason."

The witch didn't answer. She turned her head on the pillow and watched a fascinated Javala moving about the room, studying the statues and the wall hangings.

"You seem to like art, young lady."

Javala looked sheepish. "I find your collection very interesting and some of it very beautiful."

The witch chuckled again. "I admit some of the works are a trifle bizarre."

"We are pressed for time, Tajine," Zaggie said bluntly. "I suggest we put art aside for the moment and think about the talisman. Is it still in the old hiding place?"

"You are right, Zaggie. Time is running out. For me, as well. You and Hoops go this instant to the library and fetch it. Meanwhile, I'll have a chat with Javala and also have her select some cloaks from my wardrobe. You will need them on the final leg of your journey."

Zaggie led Hoops down a long corridor to Tajine's library. Immediately upon entering, candles scattered throughout the room burst into flame.

"You did that, Zaggie?"

"Of course, you silly Wiffin. I realize I face many years of study and hard work before I'll be as powerful as my twin sister, Tajine, but I've always possessed some minor talents. Lighting a bunch of candles is really quite basic."

The library shelves were stacked with ancient documents, most of them coated with a gray film of mold. The mold seemed thicker, less disturbed on one side of the room.

Zaggie must have been reading Hoop's thoughts. "Indeed, the manuscripts on that side of the room have not been used by Tajine for many years. Those are the ones that deal with the White Arts. Unfortunately, my misguided sister devoted most of her time to delving into the Black Arts even when she was a child. That's how she learned to transform me into a black cat."

"Why did she do that to you, her twin sister, no less?"

"That was the problem: we were twins. That meant we would have to share the magical power we inherited from our dear mother. Tajine wanted all the power for herself. She couldn't kill me—that's forbidden among witch siblings—but she did manage to cast a spell on me while I was sleeping. Once I was a feline, it was easy for her to banish me from Dourghoul Keep, the touchstone of my family's magical powers. I was fortunate to end up in the care of your most kind and talented grandfather."

"But Armarugh is a great sorcerer. Couldn't he teach you to become a powerful witch like your sister?" asked Hoops.

"Don't blame Armarugh. He's a good teacher, although he certainly didn't get far with you, did he?" Zaggie flashed fangs in a smile. "My powers were derived from this rather dreary castle. When I was forced to leave this ancient keep, I left behind most of what little power I possessed as a young child—or kitten. Now that I am back here, in my old home, I feel that magical strength returning. Not all at once, mind you. It'll take time."

"You're telling me that you're staying here, aren't you, Zaggie? You're not going back with me to Wiffinvolk land." He felt, for the first time perhaps, a sudden fondness for this strange little cat. For a moment, he even felt tears welling up in his eyes.

"That's right, Hoops. At any moment, I'm going to become the new Witch of Dourghoul Keep. That title puts fear into even the most hardened Lughs or Sariens."

"Will I see you again or is this going to be a permanent goodbye?"

"Don't be silly, Hoops. Of course, I'll be visiting your country quite frequently. But not until I master the art of flying. I have no intention of getting my paws wet trying to cross over Horn Harbor."

Zaggie trotted over to a cold stone fireplace and peered inside across a thick layer of ashes on the hearth. "It's the center stone in the back, if I remember correctly," she mumbled aloud. "Now, if I can remember the intonation." She thought for a few seconds before chanting a spell in a strange tongue.

The heavy stone slid out and crashed onto the hearth. A cloud of ashes billowed up into the cat's face. Zaggie cursed violently as she pawed grit from her eyes.

"That stone was supposed to float out of the cavity, not fall into the fireplace and make a mess. I must have uttered some wrong words. Indeed, I do have a lot of studying ahead of me!"

"The talisman? Is it there, Zaggie?"

"That's next," the cat replied. "Be patient. Hopefully, I'll get it right this time." She again purred in a strange fashion and out of the cavity left by the fallen stone floated a small gold box. Hoops instinctively stretched out a hand, and the box drifted gently through the air and came to rest in his open palm.

"A much better job," said a satisfied Zaggie. "Don't open the box, Hoops. Leave it be until you deliver it to your grandfather."

Hoops started to tuck the box away in the pouch dangling from his belt. Suddenly, he stopped. "Once the Lughs and Sariens hear you're the new powerful witch of Dourghoul, they won't dare trespass on your lands. The talisman will remain safe here, as it has been under Tajine's reign. So why don't you keep it? After all, Zaggie, unless I'm lucky—and I haven't been so far—I'll be captured before I've a chance to reach my ship. The talisman may well wind up in Saragata's hands."

"A distinct possibility, I agree. Your grandfather and I discussed all this at great length before we set sail for Sar. We agreed it would be preferable for you to at least try to spirit the talisman back to Wiffinvolk."

"But why?"

"For several reasons, Hoops. To begin with, my sister craved power. The very idea of holding in the palm of her hand the power to decide the fate of kingdoms made her quiver with excitement. I don't crave that power nor do I relish being burdened with the responsibility it entails.

"Secondly, in case you haven't noticed, dear Hoops, my sister changed my physical being, much like she has changed her own. She is no longer immortal. Nor am I. Who knows when the angel of death will tap me on the shoulder? I won't be around forever, Hoops, to safeguard the talisman from the clutches of either the Lughs or the Sariens. The talisman is no longer safe here."

"Then why not just let me turn the talisman over to the Queen of Sar? You heard her promise that, even with the Lughs vanquished, she would never lift a hand against Horn Harbor."

"I'm sure she means what she says, Hoops. But remember that Queen Saragata is plagued with a cough that, I understand, grows worse each day. Armarugh, Tajine, and I are convinced that the queen may not be long for this world. She's unmarried. She has no trusted children to inherit her throne. When she dies, there will be a power struggle within the palace. Who will win the throne? The likes of Itus, perhaps?" Zaggie shook her little head. "Do you think that someone like Itus will honor the deceased queen's wishes and spare Wiffinvolk from enslavement? Not likely, Hoops! Take the talisman, dear Wiffin, and try your best to deliver it safely to your grandfather."

They hurried back to Tajine's chambers to find Javala standing beside the bed, concern shadowing her face.

"She was cheerfully lecturing me about what made good art great. It was all fascinating. Then suddenly, she fell unconscious. Her breathing is very labored," Javala said. "I'm worried about her."

"I'm sure you are, Javala. But you must remember that Tajine brought this upon herself." The wolves around the bed paced back and forth nervously.

"Tajine's familiars know the end is near," Zaggie commented. "I fear that I will have to accept them as my own familiars once she's dead. I'd prefer to have cats around the castle. The gods know I've had enough trouble getting along with that silly Havoc. But I'm afraid I just can't throw these wolves out of Dourghoul. It's been their home for so long. It wouldn't be fair to them. By the way, Javala, do you have the cloaks Tajine mentioned?"

Javala picked up two neatly folded woolen cloaks from a bedside chair. "Tajine said the rose-colored one was for me. She thought it a shade too feminine for you, Hoops. Yours is the dark green one."

"Excellent!" exclaimed Zaggie. "Now, follow me to the secret passage. We'll pick up some torches on our way. Let's hurry!" She headed for the door.

Hoops, Javala, and Havoc, who appeared much relieved to escape scrutiny from Tajine's bevy of black wolves, followed the winged cat through a maze of corridors and down narrow stairwells until they reached the castle dungeons. Around a corner, they stumbled across rows of iron cages. A cacophonous chorus of moans, growls, hisses, and cries of pain greeted them. Hoops thrust his torch close to one of the cages, gasped, and jumped back. A cold sweat broke out on his forehead. The dancing torchlight reflected off an array of grotesque creatures huddled together on a pile of filthy straw. Some of the beings had human bodies, but their features were those of deformed beasts. Some had misshapen muzzles, others twisted horns, while some had reptilian eyes.

"What are these things, Zaggie?" Javala's voice trembled.

"Obviously the results of my sister's failed experiments. I didn't realize Tajine was capable of so much evil. I fear I can never restore these beings to their original forms, but I will release them from this dungeon and provide them with decent living quarters in the castle. Hopefully, I'll learn someday how to ease their misery."

Zaggie led on through several corridors until they reached a dead end of solid stone. "This is the entrance to the passage," announced Zaggie. "It will take you under the moat and about two or three furlongs further underground. You will find steps leading up to an opening atop a tree-covered knoll. I suggest you extinguish your torches before you surface on the moor. That suspicious Itus might have taken the precaution of placing guards around the entire keep instead of just mounting sentries at the drawbridge entrance."

"I don't see a doorway," said Javala.

"Patience, please," replied Zaggie. "I just have to remember the correct spell. It's been a long time since I used the incantations."

For several moments, silence reigned as Zaggie, eyes closed, appeared to be lost in concentration. From high above in the keep came the howl of a wolf. One by one, the other wolves joined in until the mournful sound reverberated throughout the fortress. The roar of the tempest outside underscored their cries.

"Tajine is dead," announced Zaggie, glancing up at the vaulted, damp ceiling. "I suppose I should be remorseful, but I'm not." She turned her attention back to the wall before them and chanted another strange incantation. A portion of the wall rolled back, revealing a low, narrow passageway. "I suggest you be on your way, now," Zaggie said. "I have to prepare for a confrontation with Itus. I believe we don't have much time before dawn awakes over the moor and he decides to come charging in here, looking for you."

"What are you going to do, Zaggie?" asked a worried Hoops. "He's capable of anything when he's angry!"

"Don't be concerned about me, Hoops. I'm the new Witch of Dourghoul Keep. I'll come up with enough magical tricks to bluff him into leaving me alone. I may even parade before his men a few of those miserable creatures in those cages we passed. I'll threaten to do the same to them if they start getting nasty with me. Surely, that'll give them pause."

Javala picked up Zaggie and gave her a big kiss on the nose. "Please take care of yourself, little witchy cat."

As soon as she put Zaggie down, the cat walked over to Havoc and rubbed her head against one of his forelegs. Havoc gave her a lick on the head. "I guess you're not such a bad wolf, Havoc," Zaggie purred. "It was probably your bad breath that bothered me the most. But it now seems I'm going to have to tolerate a lot more wolf breath, even in my bedroom." She laughed. "Now, get along you three. I have much to do, and I want to make sure this wall looks solid again once you're on your way."

"It's awfully dark in there," Javala said nervously. "It is safe, isn't it?"

"Of course, it's safe. There are some spiders and some rats and some bats, but they all are perfectly harmless."

"I can't go in there!" screeched Javala. She grabbed Hoops's hand, trembling violently. "I'm frightened to death."

"You, Javala, are afraid of something? I can't believe it. What's got you so scared?" Hoops asked incredulously.

"Bats! I'm terrified of bats!"

Hoops dragged the whimpering Javala into the secret passage.

Chapter 15

A dim, fog-shrouded dawn welcomed the trio as they emerged from the tunnel. They found themselves in the midst of dwarfed, shadowy trees atop a small knoll. The sharp odor of leaf mold and rotting vegetation permeated the thick, damp air. Javala was still shuddering. "I've never been so scared in my whole life as I was back in that passageway. I could have sworn one of those bats was going to get tangled in my hair at any moment." Havoc nuzzled her knee. Javala gradually stopped trembling and began rubbing the wolf behind its ears. "Now what do we do?" she asked Hoops.

"Havoc and I set out for the mouth of the Black River where my boat is hidden. Then, with luck and favorable winds, we sail home with the talisman."

"Is the talisman so important?"

"Yes, Javala. It could determine the fate of even your own people should it fell into the wrong hands." Hoops replied. "I suppose you will be leaving us now to find your way back to your clansmen?" Disappointment crept into his voice.

Javala tugged her rose-colored cloak tightly about her shoulders. She seemed pensive for a few moments. "No!" she said firmly. "I swore to old Yukman to accompany you until your mission is accomplished. I don't have my bow, so I'm not sure what help I can be to you. Nevertheless, I must abide by my oath to the Skagg chieftain. I believe I'll have done my duty once I've seen you and Havoc safely aboard your ship and sailing away. Then, I'll try again doubling back to my homeland. Hopefully, I'll be more successful dodging the Sariens than I was last time."

Her response buoyed Hoops's sagging spirits. "I'd be delighted to have you along for my journey to the seacoast. Havoc is a great traveling companion, but our one-sided conversations can get very boring." He knelt down and scraped fallen leaves from a small circle of damp earth. With the point of his long hunting knife, he etched a pyramid in the ground. "This represents Gauntlet Mountain," he explained to a curious Javala. He drew a line designating the seacoast. "We've got to decide what Itus will do the moment—and that could be right now—he discovers we've left Dourghoul. He won't try to pick up our trail from Dourghoul. I'm certain there are no experienced trackers among those legionnaires. Instead, he'll make for the coastline and try to head us off. By now, the general must realize I have a boat secreted somewhere along the coast. Which route will he take to get there: the one we followed to get to Dourghoul or the longer route to the east of Gauntlet Mountain?"

"The shorter route, the one we followed here," Javala answered without hesitation.

"I don't think so. He won't have you as a hostage to negotiate his way out of a certain massacre if he runs across the Skaggs again. He won't have me—or better yet, Havoc—to guide his men back through the treacherous Great Mire. That group knows nothing about the significance of the heart-shaped mushrooms. As much as you and I despise the general, he's still a professional soldier. I doubt he'd risk sacrificing those legionnaires needlessly."

Javala shook her head. "I disagree. That madman is reckless. I've overheard the legionnaires talking about him. One of them— the rather quiet soldier who lost his nose in a battle—said that Itus would lead them to certain death if he thought it would bolster his military career."

"Perhaps, you're right about that. But at the same time, the general has to contend with Gartho. The captain isn't going to tolerate anyone issuing suicidal orders to his Fourth Legionnaires. The loyalty of those men lies first with their captain. Do you see where I'm leading?"

She nodded. "If it came to a serious confrontation between Itus and Gartho, I know the legionnaires would back their captain. On return to Sar, they'd probably report that Itus suffered a *fatal accident* somewhere in the wilds. After all, if it hadn't been for your misguided intervention, he'd have had that accident already back in the Great Mire."

"I suggest we take the shorter route, assuming that Itus feels he has no choice but to take the longer one," said Hoops. "That should get us to the coast well before the legionnaires. But that doesn't give us an excuse for taking our time getting there. I wager that Itus will force march those legionnaires day and night with no breaks at all in an attempt to beat us to the coast. We'd best get on the move."

Hoops was carefully recovering his crude map with leaves and replacing his knife in its sheath when Javala commented, "You still look very worried. Are you having second thoughts about which route to take?"

"No. It's just that I'm anxious about Zaggie. I pray Itus doesn't do her any harm in a fit of anger."

Javala smiled. "Don't worry about Zaggie, little Wiffin. She's a tough and crafty cat. Or must I now say *witch*? I'm convinced she's conjured up enough terrifying magical tricks to leave all those men, even Itus, quivering in their armor."

The three silently made their way from the wooded knoll and across the fog-blanketed moor until they reached a rain-swollen stream flowing through a narrow ravine. Hoops turned upstream, certain the water flowed down from Gauntlet Mountain. The fog was so dense he had trouble getting his bearings.

They had followed the stream for almost a league when Havoc suddenly halted and spun around, sniffing at the fog surrounding them. He growled, fangs bared.

"Someone behind us?" whispered Javala.

"Certainly, Havoc heard or smelled something." Hoops felt a tingling, apprehensive sensation on the back of his neck, yet he was determined to sound calm.

"But it's not the legionnaires. Surely, you and I would have heard those heavy-footed soldiers trudging along. Most likely just a curious jackal or wolf. Don't worry about it, Javala." They reached a stand of tall cedars and climbed out of the ravine as the fog began to dissipate. Hope for a glimmer of sunlight was short-lived. A lead-hued overcast sky hung over the wintry countryside. "Let's take a short break," said Hoop. He dropped into a sitting position, his back against a tree.

Neither he nor Javala had slept for almost two days. He considered suggesting a short nap, but shrugged off that idea. They were so exhausted they might oversleep, losing precious time. Itus wasn't going to allow his men any rest until they got to the coast. "I'm starving. It's a pity we didn't collect some food supplies at Dourghoul Keep," said Javala. She was sitting against a fallen log, Havoc already asleep at her side.

Although he was several paces away from her, Hoops could hear the girl's empty stomach grumbling in protest. "I doubt Tajine had anything in her kitchen larder except chunks of raw goat and entrails." Hoops vividly recalled the carcass beside the witch's bed. He imagined Zaggie would launch her new housekeeping chores first in the kitchen. She hated goat, especially raw goat meat.

He again felt that apprehensive tingling sensation on the back of his neck. Something was lurking nearby. He glanced at Havoc. The red wolf slept peacefully, clearly unaware of any danger. Javala sat quietly with her hands folded on her bent knees, staring straight ahead. There was no hint of expression in her green eyes.

"Do you hear something moving around?" Hoops said in a half whisper.

She didn't answer. Her features remained rigid, unresponsive. Hoops realized she was in a trance. He heard the snap of a twig behind him at the edge of the ravine. He spun around. A black leopard crouched only a few feet away. The immense feline had cerulean blue eyes. Hoops sprung to his feet, shrugging off his cloak and yanking his ax free from his belt. He cocked his arm into a throwing position. The leopard snarled. Hoops could see its muscles tense, ready to spring. Hoops threw the ax. The blade slammed into the leopard's head, wedging itself deep into its skull. The creature reared up on its hind legs, screaming in anger and agony. Instantly, it burst into a pillar of yellow flames and thick black smoke. Hoops jumped back to avoid the intense heat. He tripped over a broken branch and fell backward, slamming his head hard against a fallen log. For a few moments, he lay stunned, eyes closed.

"That hurt, Wiffin! Don't ever try that again." Hoops opened his eyes to see the God of War standing over him. Brutius was balancing Hoops's belt ax in one hand and toying with his well-trimmed beard with the other. "I'm an immortal. You can't kill a Sarien deity. You should know that."

"I was trying to kill a threatening leopard."

"Ah, well. Perhaps, I should not have chosen that particular guise. But I needed to track you down quickly. As a leopard, I was able to pick up your scent easily. I suppose, as a wolf, I could have gotten the same results and perhaps not frighten you so much. But wolves are awkward animals. They lack the leopard's graceful movements."

"Why did you follow us?"

"To recover the talisman you've stolen. This is the last day of the month of Tor, and I must return to the Eternal Mountain tonight. I want to make certain Queen Saragata has that talisman before nightfall. So, hand it over this instant." The blue-eyed god extended his hand, palm up, to receive it.

Hoops shook his head vehemently. "It's not destined for the queen."

"I don't want to have to kill you, Hoops."

"A Sarien deity can't kill me, Brutius. I happen to know that."

Brutius looked perturbed. "Nevertheless, Wiffin, I can cause you so much pain that you'd wish you were dead. Don't tempt me!"

Hoops was on his feet, hunting knife in hand. "You're not getting the talisman, Brutius!"

Brutius closed his extended right hand and pointed his index finger at Hoops. A blast of cold air caught Hoops in the chest. He was thrown high into the air and slammed violently against a massive tree trunk. Pain swept throughout his body. He was certain his spine had been broken. Then he dropped to the ground only to feel another surge of pain tear at his injured right knee.

"That's just for starters, Hoops," said a self-satisfied Brutius. "You want more?"

Hoops, in agony, prone on his back and gasping for breath, felt at his belt for the little leather pouch containing the talisman. As he did so, something the witch Tajine had said about Brutius flashed through his mind. Exactly what had she said? "I guess you have won, Brutius," he said through clenched teeth, as he struggled into a sitting position. "However, before I give it to you, why don't we have a frank discussion, man-to-man?"

"I'm a god. You're a youngster. I don't believe a *man-to-man* discussion is very appropriate at this point. Please hand over the talisman before my temper frays."

"Well, how about a discussion between two civilized beings? You consider yourself civilized, don't you?"

Brutius's eyes flashed with annoyance. "Of course, you silly Wiffin. Why do you think I, the great God of War, side with the Sariens? It's because, like me, they are civilized. They know how to throw an elegant party. Not so with the barbarian Lughs! The last time I was honored at one of their feasts, they served up grilled black scorpion tails to be washed down with a horrible concoction of cheap wine and rancid camel's milk. It was simply disgraceful!"

"Indeed, Brutius, that is dreadful. That's why we, civilized beings, must look out for each other's interests," Hoops replied, hoping he sounded sincere enough. "That's why it is so imperative that you remain the much needed and much-adored Sarien god of war."

"What are you saying, Hoops? I'll always be adored by Queen Saragata and her subjects. I lead them to glorious victories. Without my help, there wouldn't be triumphal marches with prisoners in chains, the blare of trumpets, or the banners of victory waving in the breeze over that proud city. Don't forget, Hoops, that the greatest temple in the City of Sar is dedicated to me. The tallest, most magnificent statue in the palace square represents me in pure gold and in full uniform!"

"No doubt, Brutius. And we want to keep it that way, don't we?"

"I can't understand what are you talking about, Hoops. If you are simply stalling, I'm going to lose my temper and you'll regret it."

"What will the queen do with the talisman once you deliver it to her?"

"She'll use it to wipe the Lughs off the face of this planet. What did you expect her to do? It will be the final, great victory of Sar. It'll bring everlasting peace to her realm."

"That's the problem!" Hoops shouted, scrambling to his feet despite his painful knee. "Don't you see? Everlasting peace! No more wars! You'll find yourself out of a job. You'll be an unemployed god of war, and nobody lavishes taxpayers' money on monuments honoring the unemployed."

"But . . . " Brutius, red-faced, was lost for words.

"Exactly, Brutius. You're thinking the same as I. Certainly, Queen Saragata will be thankful to you for that final, grand victory over the Lughs. But people, even queens, can be fickle, their memories short-lived. Trust me, when you're no longer needed, they will turn to other gods they do need in times of peace. Don't be surprised if, after a year or so, the queen melts down your gold statue and replaces it with one dedicated to the Goddess of Grain. Or perhaps, the Goddess of the Vineyard! Now, there's a lady who loves good parties!"

An expression of horror clouded the god's eyes. He shuddered and screamed, "Enough, Wiffin! What you've said is terrible! This can't happen to a great god like me." Suddenly, tears streamed down his pale cheeks and he went into a bout of uncontrollable sobs.

"Calm yourself. Not all is lost, my dear Brutius," Hoops said reassuringly. "All can be saved if you simply let me continue on my way back to Horn Harbor with the talisman. Then, the Sariens and the Lughs will continue to be at each other's throats for centuries to come. Your services will forever be in great demand. And there'll be no end of Sarien festivities in your honor. Won't that be wonderful?" A glimmer of hope flashed across the god's tear-streaked face, but it was only momentary.

"But if Saragata ever learns that I allowed the talisman slip through my hands, she'll feel betrayed. She'll have nothing to do with me ever again." Another crying bout rattled his entire body.

"Get control of yourself, Brutius. There is no need for that to happen. Simply tell Saragata that you couldn't find me. Hopefully, Itus won't, either. She'll always believe the talisman made its way to neutral Horn Harbor, never to be used unless someone is so stupid as to try to invade the Wiffinvolk."

Brutius, still tearful, fell down on his knees before Hoops. In a plaintive voice, he pleaded, "Promise me never to tell her or anyone else. What has transpired here today. Please, Hoops! Will you swear to the gods, even to Wiffin gods, you won't do that to me?"

"I promise, Brutius," Hoops said solemnly. "Now that we've solved your problem, I strongly suggest you be on your way. You have to be on the Eternal Mountain by dark and I still have a long distance to go."

Brutius staggered to his feet. He turned his back and started walking down into the ravine. His gait was unsteady.

"Brutius," Hoops called after him. "I think you forgot something. It seems you put both Javala and my wolf into a trance. I would greatly appreciate if you would bring them out from under your spell."

Brutius nodded his head but didn't look back. He continued on his way along the edge of the gurgling stream.

Hoops looked over at Javala. She was yawning and stretching her arms above her head. Havoc was awake, cleaning his feet.

"I think be best we be on our way," Hoops said. He took a few steps but the pain in his knee was so severe he was forced to sit down again and massage the swelling joint.

"Are you alright? You look like you're in sheer agony."

"I'll be fine," he assured her, knowing full well he wouldn't be.

Chapter 16

With his ax, Hoops made a crutch from a sturdy branch, forked at one end. "We won't make good time with you hobbling along on that thing," Javala said. "Perhaps, we should stay here until tomorrow morning and give that swollen knee a good rest before you try walking on it."

Hoops shook his head. "We'd lose too much time. Itus might get ahead of us. No, we'll march for the rest of this afternoon. I keep telling you that my knee acts up like this quite often for no reason at all, but with a little exercise, it gets better quickly." He thought he sounded convincing, but from the frown on Javala's face, he realized she wasn't in the least reassured.

Havoc growled and started pawing the earth at the edge of the ravine. Javala went over to see cause of the wolf's strange behavior. "This is most unusual," she called to Hoops from the streambed. "There are big cat prints along the bank. They look fresh. Either a panther or a leopard made them. But those big predators rarely hunt the moors. They usually stay in the mountains," she added, as she climbed out of the ravine and returned to where Hoops was seated on a log.

"Maybe one strayed down from Gauntlet Mountain," suggested Hoops.

"Perhaps. But it's weird. When I was napping, I dreamed about a black leopard with, of all things, blue eyes. It was a very vivid, real-life dream."

Using his makeshift crutch, Hoops slowly rose to his feet, trying to keep his weight off his right leg. "You didn't have any other strange dreams, did you?"

"Only that you and the God of War were having a heated argument while I slept." She grinned. "He demanded the talisman, and you gave it to him."

"I did not!" Hoops blurted out. Instinctively, he squeezed the little pouch at his belt to make certain the gold box containing the talisman was still inside. It was.

"What did you just say, Hoops?" Javala's eyes narrowed with suspicion.

"Sorry for my poor choice of words. What I meant to say was that I would never give the talisman to him, under any circumstances."

"Are you keeping something from me, Wiffin?"

"Absolutely not," he protested. But from the expression in Javala's eyes, Hoops knew she didn't entirely believe him. They made poor time crossing Skagmoor. Despite the crutch, Hoops was in excruciating pain most of the time, forcing Javala to call for frequent and lengthy breaks to give his knee some rest. During one of these stops halfway across the silent moor, Havoc disappeared into the bracken for a short while. When he reappeared, he carried a small rabbit in his jaws.

Javala gave the wolf a big kiss on his muzzle. "Finally, we'll have something to nibble on tonight, thanks to you. But next time, please try to find a bigger rabbit." She threw the rabbit over her shoulder, and they continued on their way. They were within sight of the Great Mire when darkness overwhelmed the moor, and Javala insisted on calling a halt and camping for the night. "We're going to get some sleep, Hoops, and I don't want to hear any arguments from you. It's difficult enough wandering through the Great Mire in broad daylight and on two good legs. In the dark, you'd be courting disaster. Besides, I figure we're still well ahead of those legionnaires, perhaps by a full day or more," she said. She had picked a campsite beside a clear, cold brook. Using Hoops's hunting knife, she cut a bundle of dried thistle stems and bracken to build a small fire. She refused to let Hoops gut and skin the rabbit. "You seem to forget I'm a Gretien, a girl raised in the wilderness. I've been dressing wild game since I was a toddler."

While all three were gnawing on the scant roasted meat, Hoops asked Javala, "How did you manage to save Itus's horse and then find your way safely out of the Great Mire in the dark?"

"Again, you seem to forget I'm a Gretien. We are nomadic herdsmen. We know how to take care of animals, especially our valuable horses. Please don't ask me to reveal the secrets of our trade, Hoops. As for finding our way out of the Great Mire in the dark, credit goes to the horse. Horses have a keen sense of smell. Itus's stallion simply followed the scent of Gartho's mare through the swamp."

Hoops nodded. "I guess my question was silly."

Javala didn't comment. She was busy stripping stringy meat off a leg bone. She tossed the bare bone to Havoc. When nothing remained of the hare, not even bone fragments, Javala turned to Hoops and said bluntly, "Please take off your leggings."

"In front of you? Absolutely not!"

"Have it your way, then," she said. Before he realized what she was doing, she used his own knife to slice an opening in the leather around his injured knee.

"By Zob, Javala. You've just ruined the only leggings I have! What do you think you're doing?"

"Stop protesting so loudly, Wiffin. I need to look at that knee." In the flickering firelight, the swollen knee glared hot red. Javala felt around it with her slender fingers. Her touch was gentle, but still, Hoops winced with pain. "We've got to get the swelling down, Hoops. Don't you dare move that leg. I'll be right back." She disappeared into the darkness heading for the nearby stream, his knife still in her hand.

A few moments later, she returned carrying well-soaked strips of rose-colored cloth she had cut from her cloak and sprigs of some kind of herb unknown to Hoops. "These compresses are ice cold and they won't feel very pleasant at first, but they'll help reduce the swelling." She sprinkled the herbs on his knee and then bound it loosely, ignoring his protests that the compresses were stinging his inflamed joint. "I'm going to do this about every two hours while you sleep.

In the morning, I'll bind up that knee tightly to help give it better support. Havoc and I will keep watch tonight. I want you to get a good night's rest."

Hoops did not get a good night's sleep. He was jerked awake each time Javala replaced the cold compresses with even icier ones. When sleep did return to him, he was plagued with recurring nightmares. Grotesque creatures—part humans, part beasts with iron-tipped claws and flaming red eyes—pranced around him, snarling, threatening to rip him apart any moment. In their midst stood a gigantic horse. On the stallions back sat Itus, holding the reins in his iron claw. The scar tissue, where he once had an ear, glared an angry crimson. His craggy features twisted in a triumphal grin. Hoops awoke in a cold sweat. Bright sun blinded him momentarily. Javala, with Havoc by her side, sat on a boulder close by. With a piece of charred thistle stem, she was intently sketching something on a gray, flat rock resting on her knees.

"What are you drawing?"

Javala glanced up, startled. "So, you're finally awake." She smiled. "Leg feels better?"

Hoops gingerly touched the bandaged knee. It was tender. He bent the joint gently. It was stiff, but there was no bolt of searing pain. "It's much better, thanks to you. Are you going to show me what you've drawn?"

"No. I'm afraid you'll laugh." She dropped the piece of charcoal and appeared about to erase the drawing with the heel of her fist. But Hoops stopped her.

"Please don't rub it off, Javala. Please show me. I promise I won't laugh."

Javala looked embarrassed. After a moment's hesitation, she held the rock up for Hoops's viewing.

"By Zob, you've drawn me!"

Javala giggled nervously. "Let's just say I tried to draw you. I realize it isn't very good."

"It's excellent. I admit, however, you've made me look awfully tired with big circles under my eyes. Do I really look that bad?"

"I'm afraid so, Hoops. You need more rest."

Hoops glanced up at the sun. "It's past midmorning, Javala. You shouldn't have let me sleep this long. We've lost valuable time."

"I'm sure we're still way ahead of those foot soldiers, Hoops. Besides, you really didn't have a restful night. I woke you up each time I changed the compresses. And the rest of the night, you were having bad dreams. I could tell from your constant mutterings about evil monsters and General Itus on horseback."

Hoops slammed his fist against his forehead. "I forgot about Itus!"

"What do you mean, Hoops? How could you forget about that one-eared fiend?"

"He's on horseback, Javala. Why am I so stupid! Why didn't I think of that before? He's probably left Gartho and the foot soldiers far behind and is riding at full gallop for the coastline. He'll simply round up soldiers from garrisons along the seacoast and start the search for us from there. My grandfather always thought I was stupid, and he was so right!"

Javala looked shocked. She was silent for several seconds, then exclaimed, "Don't blame yourself, Hoops. I was the one who was stupid. I'm from a land where we spend our lives on horseback. It should have dawned on me immediately what Itus might do. Once more, I'm to blame!"

"It's likely Itus already is well ahead of us," Hoops said angrily. "We've lost too much time because of this knee of mine. I'll wager legionnaires will be swarming all over us the moment we exit the Great Mire. It's too risky for us to continue on."

"Too risky?" Javala shouted in frustration. "What do you intend to do, Hoops? Abandon your all-important mission? Are you going to simply sit here, trembling in your boots and praying to your little god, Zob, that the Sariens so fear the Great Mire and the Skaggs that they won't come looking for you eventually? Don't count on that, Hoops. Both the queen and General Itus are very determined people. They're certainly not cowards!"

"Don't call me a coward!" Hoops screamed back.

"Then prove it, Wiffin! Get on your feet this very instant!"

"We aren't going! I'm going, but not you, Javala. Do I make myself clear?"

"What are you talking about?" She spat at him, clenching her fists.

"It's too dangerous for you to accompany me, you hot-tempered, irritating Gretien. If the soldiers catch you this time, you're dead. No question about that. I'm a Wiffin, a foreigner. With some fast talking and a great deal of sheer luck, I might get away with just a lifetime sentence in a cozy Sarien dungeon."

"What do you expect me to do, Hoops, just abandon you out here?" Javala had lowered her voice, but it still reflected an undercurrent of rage.

"I expect you to go in search of Yukman. The Skaggs will guarantee you safe passage to find your clansmen. After all, Javala, you have your own mission to carry out. You've already helped me all you can."

Javala stared at Hoops with an expression of disbelief in her green eyes. "I can't believe what I'm hearing. I've helped you? By the gods, Hoops, I've caused you nothing but trouble so far. If it hadn't been for me, you'd already have your precious talisman and be sailing off to your homeland."

She suddenly burst into laughter. "You have a knack for saying the most ridiculous things, Hoops. Yes, I have my own mission." She turned serious again. "Yukman tells me that my foolish brother, who's acting chief of our clan, wants to negotiate a truce with Queen Saragata. I can't imagine what's gotten into his head, but I'll not tolerate it. She made war on us. I'll make war on her!"

"Then go, Javala, and do your duty."

"Be assured I'll do my duty, Hoops. But only after I've seen you safely on your delightful ship and on your way home. Don't forget, I swore an oath to Yukman. We, Gretiens, always honor our oaths." She smiled. "Now, please let's get moving." She handed him his crutch, turned, and started across the moor in the direction of the Great Mire. Havoc followed at her heels.

Chapter 17

Eddies of pale yellow-gray mist twisted and twirled in a macabre ballet about them as they ventured through the Great Mire. Hoops no longer relied heavily on his makeshift crutch. His knee remained stiff, but the excruciating pain had faded. "I don't know how you did it, Javala, but you worked magic on my leg."

"It was just an old Gretien remedy we use when our horses get a sprain. I'm still going to insist we take several rest stops. I doubt that Itus, even if he's ridden ahead of us, has been able to organize search parties this quickly." She spoke with confidence. Hoops remained skeptical. He had memorized the map of Sar which Arrnarugh had rolled out on a candlelit table when they plotted Hoops's journey to Dourghoul Keep. There were Sarien garrisons stationed at each fishing village along the coast, all within less than an hour's ride from each other. If Itus reached just one of those hamlets, orders to organize a search could be spread very rapidly the length of the coastline. The coastal plain was an open, flat grassland offering few places to hide from patrolling legionnaires on horseback. To reach his boat secreted in the Black River delta, they had no choice but to cross the coastal plain. The Great Brambles, a wedge-shaped expanse of interwoven thorn bushes and briars, blocked any other approach to the river. Armarugh claimed that nothing, not even a slithering serpent, could traverse the impregnable Great Brambles.

By late afternoon, they were several leagues deep into the Great Mire. Suddenly, Javala clutched Hoops's arm tightly. "Hear that?"

she whispered. From somewhere in the mist came a muffled moan followed by a refrain of hideous screams.

"Ghoulvats," Hoops whispered back. "We must have journeyed too close to their tomb. I thought we were on a course well away from that cursed place. We're going to have to make an even greater detour. Meaning, more lost time!" He signaled a direction change to Havoc who promptly veered off to scout a new trail through the swamp. Gradually, the cries of the Ghoulvats faded in the distance, and Hoops felt it was safe enough to again resume their original course through the mire. But the loss of more time weighed heavily on his mind.

"Don't look so gloomy, Hoops. We're going to make it to your little ship, unless we starve to death first. I've never been so hungry in my life."

"Be assured, Javala, that you're not the only one feeling hunger pains. Once we get out of this mire, perhaps we'll run across some game."

"Shouldn't we be exiting this awful swamp not far from that hamlet where we stopped on our way to Dourghoul? I recall that the old woman tavern keeper made a delicious bison stew."

Hoops shook his head. "It may not be safe for us to waltz into that tavern. It might be full of legionnaires."

"We can always scout it out first before we march in. My stomach tells me it's worth a try." Havoc again spotted a line of heart-shaped mushroom in the middle of the trail they were pursuing, and they lost more time backtracking to avoid the quicksand.

Night draped its clammy black mantle over the Great Mire and, despite Hoops's protests, Javala insisted on making camp. They built a small fire to ward off the chill, and as they huddled around it, Javala retrieved her piece of charcoal from inside her jerkin and looked around for something to draw upon. Finding nothing suitable, she looked frustrated.

"Do you do a lot of drawing back home?"

She shook her head. "We, Gretiens, are hardworking, practical people. We love reading and storytelling and reciting our ancient sagas but, otherwise, we don't find time for frivolities."

"We, Wiffins, even an untalented oaf like me, don't think of art as frivolous."

"I didn't mean to offend you or your Wiffin countrymen, Hoops," Javala said sheepishly. "If I did, I sincerely apologize."

"No offense taken. It just so happens that, in my humble opinion, you have real artistic talent. If you ever come to Wiffinvolk, my people will encourage you to develop that talent, not hide it."

"I'm afraid, Hoops, I'll probably never get an opportunity to visit your land. There are many Sariens to be killed. Revenge might take a long time." She pulled his cloak tightly about her and leaned back against a tree trunk. "Now, let's try to sleep."

Hoops dreamed that someone was nearby, watching him. He woke to a pallid dawn struggling desperately to penetrate the swaths of mist hovering over the mire. The dream persisted. Hoops silently got to his feet, pulling his ax from his belt. "Who's out there?" he demanded of the mist.

"Don't be alarmed. Tis just me, yer ol' friend, the hunter. Seems our paths have crossed again, little Wiffin."

Hoops could not see anyone in the surrounding gloom, but he recognized the lyrical, almost musical voice. "What are you doing here?"

"Hunting, of course. I sense the mission to Dourghoul Keep was a raving success, and now you're on yer merry way to the Black River?"

"How do you know where we're going, hunter?" The hunter softly chucked. "Judging from the hunting knife and that ax, I reckon you're a hunter like me. But from your deep suntan and those sea boots you're sporting, seems you've spent a bit of time on the open sea. Reckon, if I came to Sar from Horn Harbor and didn't relish having my ship found by curious Sarien legionnaires, I'd have run it into the Black River and tucked it away out of sight somewhere in the delta. I'd wager it would take those legionnaires weeks of scouring that vast maze of narrow guts and backwater canals before they discovered it."

"So, you're right. I did hide my little vessel in the delta. So what? What's that got to do with you, hunter?" Hoops said testily.

A shadowy apparition concealed in a black, hooded cloak and carrying a hunting bow in the crook of an elbow glided out of the swirling fog just a few paces from Hoops.

"Well, I just thought I'd do you a wee favor and tell you that, since you and your companions here are so popular, Lord General Itus himself wants to meet you all. Word is that he's alerted those fancy dress legionnaires all up and down the seacoast to keep a sharp eye out for the three of you. Hear tell he's even offered a reward in real gold for information as to yer whereabouts." Hoops felt his empty stomach churning. It wasn't from hunger. The hunter cleared his throat. "Mind you, don't look so dejected. I don't mean to affront you, but you seem a bit too easily discouraged. It strikes me you've got a smattering of good sense. I'm sure you'll find a way out of this."

"Don't you dare lecture me about being dejected, hunter. I've been plagued by nothing but problems this whole journey. I've a right to be discouraged!"

"Well now, laddie, look at the bright side. If I found myself no longer having to face a few problems now and again, I'd have to conclude I was laid out in me grave. You got problems? That just means you're still alive. There's something to be thankful for!"

"I don't welcome your clever comments. You just told me the legionnaires are already searching for us. I was praying we still had time to make it across the coastal plain to the delta."

"Crossing the coastal plain may be a shade risky. There must be another way to the delta. Let me get my little brain working and see what I might suggest." The hunter stood silent for a moment, trying to look as if he was lost in deep thought.

But Hoops didn't believe the charade. "Well?" he said impatiently. "May I suggest ye cut through the Great Brambles to the delta? No soldiers are going to wander into that impassable tangle of thorns looking for yer."

"That's a crazy suggestion, hunter. My grandfather says not even a snake could get through the Great Bramble."

"Indeed, your grandfather said that, did he? Well, methinks this time your grandfather might just be a wee bit wrong," said the hunter, chuckling. "If you stay out of sight and sneak past the hamlet of Vecka, where we first met, and then follow the road a scant distance further on, you'll see a tower of granite rearing up above the tree line. That marks the beginning of the Great Brambles. At the base of that rock, you'll find a tunnel entrance. It's well hidden by brush. Nobody but ignorant me knows about it. Once through that tunnel, you'll come out on a trail used for centuries by forest beasts parading back and forth 'tween here and the Black River. Follow that trail, and I'll guarantee you'll get to the delta in safety." The apparition turned and started back into the mist.

"Hold, hunter!" It dawned on Hoops that the hunter, in his torn, faded cloak and well-worn boots, could readily use a fistful of gold. Hoops sensed a trap. "Why are you telling me all this, hunter? You owe me no favors."

"Maybe I believe that everyone owes someone a favor from time to time." Again, a soft, whimsical laugh. "And by the way, please give me old friend, Armarugh, my very best regards when ye next lay eyes on him." The dark form slipped away into the fog-enveloped dawn.

Hoops was unnerved. He couldn't move for several minutes. Finally, he turned his attention to Javala and Havoc. The Gretien was curled up tightly in her flowing cloak, clearly asleep. Havoc snored peacefully in a hollow he had pawed out for himself under a fallen log. "Wake up, both of you!" Hoops yelled hoarsely. "I can't believe you two slept through my conversation with the hunter. We weren't whispering. In fact, we were talking loudly."

Javala jerked to a sitting position, throwing her cowl back and rubbing her eyes. "What's happening?"

"You didn't hear me talking with the hunter?"

"What are you talking about, Hoops? What hunter?" Havoc stared at Hoops, mystified.

"How could you have slept through all that?" Hoops demanded.

"I do believe that lack of food has played games with your senses, Hoops. Forgive me, but we, Gretiens, are naturally light sleepers. We're always attuned to sounds alerting us of dangers to our herds. I'm convinced you're imagining things. It's your empty tummy to blame, I'm sure."

"I can't believe this," Hoops mumbled to himself. But he began to have serious doubts. Did he imagine his encounter with the hunter? Was it a dream? He shook his head in bewilderment, as he watched Javala and Havoc sluggishly get to their feet. Less than an hour later, they emerged from the mist to find themselves on the edge of a wind-ruffled meadow of withered brown grass separating the Great Mire from a forest of tall cedars a furlong away. A canopy of turbulent dark clouds hung over the land. Hoops took several deep breaths of crisp, cold air to clear his lungs of the foul, decay-ridden air of the mire. Javala scanned the sky and turned to Hoops. "It's going to snow soon."

She was probably right, he thought. Now he had to pray that they would make it to the Great Brambles before the snow began. The tracks of two humans and a wolf would be spotted easily by any observant legionnaire on patrol. "Let's quickly cross over this meadow to those woods. I don't want to be caught out in the open by any Sarien soldiers who might just happen to be in the area. We're not too far from Vecka. We'll work around that hamlet, and it shouldn't be much further till we're safe in the Great Brambles."

"I hope you know what you're doing, Hoops. I am still convinced that your hunter friend, whom you've been talking about ever since we broke camp this morning, is simply a figment of your imagination. I've never heard of anyone or anything making it through the Great Brambles."

"For all our sakes, Javala, let's hope he does exist and told me the truth about that secret trail. Otherwise, we're all going to be in serious trouble."

Javala threw back the hood of her cloak and busied herself sweeping her long, wind-teased red hair back over her ears and fastening it in a ponytail. "I just hope you're right, Wiffin."

They started jogging across the meadow, Havoc loping well out in front. The wolf disappeared momentarily from view halfway across the meadow. He reappeared and stood motionless, waiting for them to catch up. "Must be a streambed or gully just ahead," Hoops remarked.

"Hold it!" Javala stopped abruptly and dropped prone to the ground, pressing an ear hard against the earth. "I thought I sensed something wrong," she said in a half whisper. "Horses heading our way. At full gallop."

Hoops glanced back over his shoulder. They were now already too far from the Great Mire to seek safety there. "The gully's our only chance!" Javala scrambled to her feet, and the two of them bent over to lower their profile, darted across the meadow and slid down an embankment to the bottom of a dry streambed. Havoc joined them, silent but with lips curled, fangs showing. Hoof beats were clearly audible now. Hoops drew his ax from his belt. His hand shook. The thunder of hooves grew louder, but the horsemen seemed to be passing them by.

"They never spotted us," Javala said in a relieved half whisper.

"Thanks, Zob," Hoops muttered. Suddenly, the morning air was rent by a chorus of howls.

"Dogs! They've got hunting dogs!" exclaimed Hoops. "And the dogs have picked up our sent!"

He felt Javala's hand reach for his belt. In an instant, she had drawn his long-bladed hunting knife from its sheath and, holding it in a professional knife fighter's fashion, said in a cold voice, "I plan to kill at least two of them before they kill me." Hoops knew she meant it.

Chapter 18

"The dogs are heading for that gully yonder!" one of the horsemen yelled. "Wheel around and follow the hounds." The rumble of the galloping horses drew closer. From the sound, Hoops guessed there were at least a dozen riders. He and Javala would not stand a chance against such odds. Surrender would be his best course of action, but he realized Javala was going to fight to the death no matter what he did. He couldn't bring himself to abandon her now. He cocked his arm, ready to throw his ax the moment a rider came into view at the edge of the gully. Javala, knife held well out in front of her body, was crouched, ready to spring. Havoc sprang first.

In a single leap, the wolf cleared the top of the embankment and sprinted off across the meadow straight at the approaching horsemen.

"It's a damn wolf!" shouted a horseman. "It just raced past me, heading for the Great Mire. The dogs are on its heels."

"Call off yours dogs, you idiot soldier. We're not hunting wolves. Besides, that's a big wolf. It's liable to turn on those stupid hounds and grind them into sausage meat if they try to corner it in that blasted swamp!" The voice was guttural, very much in charge. There came a short blast from a hunting horn, followed by another and another.

"No use. Fool dogs aren't responding. They're still after that beast, and it's already entered the swamp." A string of obscenities followed. The rumble of hooves and the shouts of the frustrated soldiers receded slightly, as the riders swung away from the gully and headed for the edge of the mire. The cries of the soldiers suddenly were drowned out by yelps of agonized pain from the hounds. Hoops heard a soldier yell, "I see those crazy dogs now. They're flying out of the mire, tails between their legs. Guess they got a shade too close to that wolf and it decided to turn around and take 'em on. A couple of those hounds look in pretty bad shape."

"They won't be worth spider's spit as trackers for the rest of this day," roared the leader. "We'd better round them up and get them back to the fort and patched up."

"Thought you said there was supposed to be a tame wolf with those youngsters we're after. Maybe that was their wolf?" Hoops recognized the voice of the soldier who had blown the horn.

"That was no tame wolf, you fool," replied the leader. "This countryside is full of wolves. Your stupid dogs jumped a wild one. Must say, you're a lousy dog trainer."

Hoops and Javala didn't stir from their hiding place until they could no longer hear the horses or the yelps of the wounded dogs. They scrambled out of the streambed and swiftly made for the shelter of the forest opposite the mire.

"What about Havoc?" Javala asked in a worried tone, as they began making their way through the trees. "He did a brave thing, saving our lives."

"He'll be along soon, Javala. Don't worry about that big critter." He added, "I must admit, I didn't know he could be so mean. He's always been so timid, fearful of most everything. Guess, you never really know what beasts—or people, for that matter—are capable of doing when they're cornered."

Havoc, slightly bloodied but enthusiastic, caught up with them as they topped a wooded rise overlooking the little hamlet of Vecka. Javala patted the wolf on the head. "You did a brave thing back there, Havoc. Seems you saved our lives." The wolf wagged his tail. The tavern where he had first met the hunter was almost directly below them. The shabby village itself lay about a hundred yards further away. It looked deserted.

"We've got to circle around the hamlet unseen and work ourselves through the woods following alongside the road until we reach that rock yonder." Hoops pointed to a pillar of stone jutting high above the treetops in the distance. "That's the way into the Great Brambles."

"Maybe it would be prudent for us to stay in these woods until dark, then go on," said Javala. "That would give me enough time to put together a bow and some makeshift arrows with crude arrowheads from flaked flint, if I can find some here. I thought about doing that earlier, but there was no wood on Skagmoor and all the wood in the Great Mire was too brittle or too rotten. At least here, we've got cedars. Cedar makes for very poor bows, but it's better than nothing. I want something more than just a hunting knife if we stumble into legionnaires once more."

Hoops nodded, but promptly changed his mind. "Listen to me carefully, Javala. Once Havoc and I are on the trail through the Great Brambles, we'll safely reach my fishing boat in the delta. Then it'll be only a question of waiting for the right wind and tide one night before we make our run for the open sea. I'll—"

Javala interrupted. "The Sariens might blockade all the inlets and rivers including the Black River to prevent you from escaping."

Hoops grinned. "I wouldn't be surprised if they do. But Sarien warships are designed for open sea battles with the Lugh navy. They aren't rigged to sail close to the wind, and they draw too much water to operate around all the sandbars and shoals fanning out from the mouth of the Black River. Besides, my grandfather swears the Sariens are rather poor sailors." Javala still looked worried. "Stop frowning, Javala. I'll give them the slip easily enough."

"I hope you're right, Hoops. Still, I can't help but worry about you."

Hoops drew a deep breath and said emphatically, "I don't need your help any longer, Javala. I want you to travel south from here, skirt the Great Mire, and strike out for the Skagmoor and find your friend, Yukman. There is no need for you to accompany me to the Black River. That would only add days to your return journey and could prove most dangerous. Please, go home now."

Javala, sitting with her back to a tree, did not look at him. She looked down at her hands folded in her lap, a hint of sadness in her green eyes. "Remember, I swore an oath to Yukman," she muttered.

"I know. But I believe you've now fulfilled your oath." Havoc trotted over to Javala and sat down beside her. She began caressing the wolf's muzzle. "I believe Havoc will miss me, Hoops."

"I know he will. I expect him to be pining for you long after we've arrived in our homeland. He's become quite fond of his young warrior friend."

She smiled, then turned serious once more. "I suppose you are right, Hoops. From here, I probably could work my way around that dreadful swamp and reach Skagmoor in two days, or three at the most. I really must search out my brother and have a very serious chat with that silly boy as soon as possible." She got to her feet, but immediately bent over in pain, hands on her stomach.

"What's wrong?" Hoops asked nervously.

Javala straightened up. She tried to smile. "Nothing serious. Just a temporary sharp pain in the tummy. It's pure hunger. I'm afraid eating just a third of a little rabbit in many days isn't enough for me. Which reminds me, Hoops. May I take your hunting knife? I'm not a bad knife thrower even with something so unbalanced as your blade, and I'll need to kill some kind of game on my journey to find Yukman. Otherwise, I'll starve to death before I locate the Skaggs."

"Certainly, you may have it, Javala." He reached for his sheath knife, but Javala abruptly grabbed his elbow.

"Smell that?" she exclaimed. "It's food cooking!"

Hoops sniffed the air. She was right. An aroma of meat roasting over a cherrywood fire drifted up toward them from below. From the tavern's crumbling stone chimney, breeze-shredded whiffs of pale blue smoke were faintly visible.

"By the great heavens, Hoops, let's go down there and see if we can get something to eat. I don't see anyone lurking around. Certainly, no soldiers. Not even a scrawny dog."

"This hamlet's so poverty-ridden, I wager they've already eaten their dogs. In fact, dog meat may be what we're smelling."

"I don't care if it's roasted bat meat. I could wolf down anything at this point in my life," Javala said. She still had a tight grip on Hoops's arm. "We could sneak down there and check out the tavern and the stables. There are plenty of cracks and holes in the walls of that building. If it's just the old lady in there, there's no reason we couldn't buy some food and be on our way immediately."

"You're insane, Javala. The hunter said there was a reward, in gold, no less, for information about us. You can bet that old woman will report us to the first legionnaire she sees."

"So, what? We'll be long gone before that happens. Even if she's got a horse in that stable and knows how to ride it, I'm sure it would take her quite a while to reach the nearest legionnaire fort to report us. We'll have disappeared by the time the soldiers got here."

Hoops ran his fingers through his unruly mop of hair. "I don't know about this, Javala. We may be taking an unnecessary risk."

"Listen, Hoops," the girl said. "I'll check the stable while you take a peek into the tavern proper. If there are any horses in the stable or you see anyone but the old lady, and maybe that young boy helper in the tavern, we'll call this off. Otherwise, we walk into the tavern, order food, and promptly leave to go our separate ways."

"Only a moment ago, Javala, you were suggesting it would be safer if we waited till nightfall to work our way around this miserable hamlet. Now you're insisting we march right into it in broad daylight and order dinner. I'm beginning to wonder if your empty stomach isn't affecting your sanity!"

Despite doubts fluttering in his mind, Hoops recognized Javala was right about one thing: if they got in and out quickly enough, there would be scant opportunity for the old woman to get timely word to the legionnaires. He and Javala should be well on their ways, heading in opposite directions. Once into the Great Brambles, he would be safe from any search, and Javala would be doubling back toward Skagmoor. No legionnaires would venture there. Itus would focus his search between the hamlet and the seacoast. His own growling stomach urged him to take the risk. *Besides,* Hoops thought. *Javala clearly was more affected by lack of food than he was.* He worried that hunger might cloud her judgment if she encountered a tight situation on her way to Skagmoor. And there was another factor to consider: no matter how good she was with a knife, he doubted she could hunt down a meal before she ever found her Skagg friends who could be anywhere in that vast moor.

"Agreed, Javala. But with reluctance and only on the condition there are no horses in the stable and there's only the old lady and her assistant in the tavern." He opened his leather belt pouch. "I've got a few coins. When we were here before, I recall the old lady made Gartho pay for our meal with salt."

"She surely will take a few coins for two chunks of roasted meat. I mean, three chunks. Don't forget Havoc needs to eat, too."

Before they started down the wooded hillside toward the tavern, Hoops removed his sheathed knife from his belt and handed it to Javala. "Just in case something happens and we have to split up in a hurry, I want you to have this."

"Thank you." She smiled and stuck the sheath into the waistband of her leggings, out of view beneath her shaggy fur jacket and cloak. "Hopefully, someday, I'll have a chance to give it back to you."

She patted Havoc on the head and gave Hoops a kiss on the cheek. They slipped silently downhill through the undergrowth.

The tavern was situated about twenty paces from the thicketed edge of the hillside. After ordering Havoc to stay put, Hoops sprinted across the muddy, open ground and reached the exterior wall of the dilapidated structure. Javala, meanwhile, had circled around to the back of the building to check the stable. Several planks in the tavern wall had separated. Through the cracks, he could see most of the dimly lit interior. A few crude whale oil lamps were scattered around on empty tables. The old woman, her back to Hoops, was bent over, stoking a cooking fire on a corner hearth. No one else was visible. The smell of smoke and roasting meat was pungent.

Javala silently joined him. She whispered, "I couldn't see much of the interior of the stable. Too dark. But there are no horses in there."

"You are certain?" Hoops whispered back.

"Trust me, Hoops. I'm a Gretien. If there was a horse in there, I'd know it. I could smell it from fifty paces away."

Hoops nodded. "Then, let's go in. There's just the old woman in the tavern, not even her helper." They straightened up from their crouched positions and walked around the corner of the rickety building and through the open tavern door. At first, the old woman appeared unaware of their presence. She remained at the fireplace, poking at the burning faggots. Hoops coughed politely. Startled, she spun around, aged eyes squinting through the smoky haze.

"What can I do you for?" she asked suspiciously.

"We were hoping to get bit of food. Whatever you're cooking smells very good."

"It's jackal. Our village hunter killed it this very morning. Want ale, too?"

"Just water would be fine."

"Water bucket's in yonder corner," she said, gesturing to a far corner opposite the fire. "Water ain't free."

Hoops nodded. "I have a few coins."

"Better have, lad. I don't run no charity house here." She sounded annoyed. Hoops guessed it was because they hadn't ordered the more expensive ale.

"How much jackal will ye be needing?"

"Three pieces," Javala answered. Hoops could tell from Javala's expression that jackal was not her favorite food, but her empty stomach ignored her taste buds.

"Three chunks, eh? Got a friend outside?"

"A dog," Hoops said, as he poured rancid water from the bucket into two wooden drinking bowls. "It's hungry, too."

"Want to sell the dog? Folks around here like dog, especially when they ain't much else for eating. Dog tastes a whole lot better than jackal."

Hoops shook his head. The woman grabbed a long, greasy knife off a nearby tabletop, wiped the blade with a corner of her dirt-streaked shawl, and quickly sliced off three portions of charred meat. She dropped them into a scum-lined bowl and started to hand it to Hoops but hesitated. "How much you got in coin, young fellow? Let me see your money first."

Hoops removed his pouch from his belt and probed inside with his fingers. He finally extracted two pieces of silver and held them out in his open palm to the woman. She flashed a toothless grin, snatched the coins, and handed Hoops the meat. "Use any table you want," she said, waving her bony hand around the room. "We ain't crowded this gloomy afternoon."

"If you don't mind, we'll take the meat with us and eat while we're traveling. We have a ways to go before nightfall, and I suspect we'll have snow before this day is over."

"And where might you be going?" Her pointed question didn't come as a surprise.

"To the City of Sar," Hoops replied nonchalantly.

"Aye, so ye's going to pay homage to our lovely queen, is ye? She'll be charmed, I'm sure." Her voice cracked with mirth. Then, her tone suddenly turning sullen, she said, "I'm thinking I've seen ye before, young lad. Yer lady friend, too, if I ain't mistaken." She squinted hard at both Hoops and Javala and announced in a loud, rasping voice, "I knew it. Ye two stopped here a short while back with a band of legionnaires. Ye had bison stew. Ye two must be the Wiffin and the Gretien girl prisoner everyone's looking for!"

The hanging canvass covering the door to the adjoining stable was ripped aside by several legionnaires who exploded into the room, wrestling Javala to the dirt floor before she could draw the hunting knife. Hoops sensed movement behind him. He spun around. A tall, bulky figure in a black cloak stood in the tavern doorway, blocking out the gray afternoon light. The man threw back the hood of his cloak, revealing a livid white scar where an ear had once been.

"I'm so pleased to see you once again, Hoops," said General Itus softly, a demonic, triumphant smile playing across his tortured features.

Chapter 19

Queen Saragata sat stern-faced and silent in a high backed, ebony chair beside a blazing hearth, studying the gold talisman case cradled in one hand. With the other, she clutched a pale lavender handkerchief.

"And that finishes my report, Your Majesty," Itus concluded. "The property that is rightfully yours has been returned. As to the prisoners, I suggest you have but one choice—death."

"Wonderful, simply wonderful!" screeched a bouncing Scotus. "But I do recommend you allow me a brief interview with them in my chamber. On the other hand, little Wiffin, I am prepared to listen to any defense you might offer. Torments before we roast them alive. My vastly improved rack needs to be tested more thoroughly and I—"

The queen turned to the inquisitor and snapped, "Silence, Scotus! When I want your advice, I'll ask for it." Scotus scurried to a darkened corner of the queen's private office. No one spoke for a few moments, while a servant entered the room with an armful of wood to replenish the fire. When he finished, he bowed to the queen and left.

The queen looked at Javala in chains, with Havoc at her side. "You have heard the charges Itus has brought against you. Are you going to say anything in your defense or, once again, remain silent?"

Javala spat on the stone floor.

"I see," Saragata said. A tone of sadness underscored her voice. "You are leaving me with no choice this time, young Gretien."

136

The queen paused to cough into her handkerchief. She shifted her gaze to Hoops. "I know the Wiffin ambassador to my court will lodge a protest, but I see no other option but to condemn you to death. You betrayed my trust and attempted to steal my property." She weighed the gold box in her hand. "On the other hand, little Wiffin, I am prepared to listen to any defense you might offer."

Hoops had anticipated this moment. Throughout a raging blizzard on the journey from the Hamlet of Vecka to the palace, he had agonized over what to say. He had struggled to reconstruct the remarks Gartho had made when, walking beside the iron-jawed captain, Hoops had first entered the City of Sar. Tajine's deathbed comments also had battled for clarity amid a torrent of confused thoughts.

"I was only trying to do you a favor, Your Highness."

The queen stared at him in disbelief. "I've never heard anyone make such a ludicrous statement under life-or-death circumstances such as these! Fear must have such firm grip on your mind that you're reduced to uttering pure gibberish."

"I am sorely afraid, Your Majesty. Anyone in my situation would be. But please believe me, I sincerely meant what I said."

"By the heavens, you do indeed appear to be serious. Would you please explain yourself?"

"I will do so, but I request a private audience with Your Highness."

The queen bounded to her feet. "Never have I heard such insolence. You, a prisoner facing death come dawn, demanding a private audience from a queen? Ridiculous!"

Saragata turned to Itus and in a furious voice, ordered the general to escort Hoops and Javala immediately to the dungeons. Havoc, she decreed, was destined for the royal menagerie. Legionnaires grabbed Hoops and Javala and roughly shoved them toward the door. Hoops could hear Itus's laughter and giggles of glee from little Scotus.

"This is no laughing matter, Itus!" the queen hissed. "You may consider yourself above such emotions, General, but I lay sleepless many a night doubting the wisdom of my decisions regarding the fate of others."

"As for you, Scotus, if I hear any more nonsense from you, you'll find yourself stretched out on your own precious rack! Do I make myself clear?"

One of the legionnaires had wrenched open the chamber doors and the soldiers were dragging the prisoners into the narrow, vaulted corridor, when the queen shouted after them, "Hold! Bring the Wiffin back in here."

Hoops found himself once more standing before the queen. His legs were trembling. Despite a chill in the room, beads of cold sweat trickled down his forehead.

"Very well, Wiffin. Before you die, I want to hear what you had to say to me. Something about a favor?"

"If you please, Your Majesty. I did not *demand* a private audience. I simply requested one." His voice, too, was trembling uncontrollably.

The queen did not respond immediately. She sat down, straightened out her flowing black silk robe, and fidgeted with loose strands of long black hair. She glanced down once more at the gold box in her hand, then raised her angry eyes to Hoops's.

"Your request is granted, Wiffin." She promptly barked orders to Itus to have everyone, including himself, leave the room.

Itus protested. The Wiffin might try to escape. Itus could not allow any harm to befall his sovereign. Didn't her majesty realize that even a little Wiffin could be dangerous when cornered, facing certain death?

"Spare me all that, Itus," Saragata retorted angrily. "I've a sword at hand. The Wiffin is in chains. My people do not hail me as the warrior queen for no reason at all. I'll handle this, thank you. Now leave us."

Itus, muttering obscenities under his breath, left the room, slamming the thick oaken doors behind him. For several moments, neither Saragata nor Hoops spoke. Only the crackling of the fire and the sporadic hissing of a few torches in iron sconces scattered about on the tall chamber walls disturbed the silence. The pungent scent of hardwood burning on the hearth was pleasant to Hoops. His mind wandered. Would he glean any last moment satisfaction from the smell of burning wood when they began roasting him alive? Most probably not.

"Well, Wiffin?"

Hoops was slow to answer. He first prayed silently. "Please, Zob, I need all the help you can bestow on your most faithful Wiffin."

The queen began tapping her silver-slippered foot impatiently. "Are you going to explain what you meant when you mentioned doing me a favor? Or are you just wasting my time?"

"If I recall, Your Majesty, only a few minutes ago, you had to remind the great Lord General Itus that your loyal subjects hail you as the Warrior Queen of Sar. That is a most impressive and certainly well-deserved title! It is evident your subjects love you dearly, and rightfully so."

Unexpectedly, the queen's eyes reflected a touch of humor. "Do not attempt to flatter me, Wiffin. Indeed, I am a warrior queen and very proud it. But I'm not such a conceited fool as to believe a title of respect is necessarily a title of love. To the contrary, Wiffin, by no means am I loved by all my subjects. Perhaps, many of my Sariens looked upon me with some affection. But Sar is a vast kingdom. An empire, really. It's a conglomerate of diverse nations, tribes, and clans, even little rival kingdoms. Many are fiercely independent minded and resent my power over them. Indeed, Wiffin, I would require an elaborate abacus to calculate just how many enemies I have."

Saragata paused to again cough into her handkerchief. "Certainly, your Gretien friend is one. She would rather put an arrow through my heart than curtsy." The queen became pensive, her eyes fixed on Hoops but seeing through him as if he didn't exist. "Perhaps, the girl is justified in her hatred. I don't really know how the incident with the Gretiens came about. I must accept Itus's version of what happened. He is, after all, my lord general. Hopefully, I can reestablish good relations with the Gretiens despite this tragedy."

Hoops nodded solemnly. "A tragedy it was, indeed, Your Majesty. But we must not dwell on the past. We must now focus on the future—your future and that of your majestic kingdom!"

The queen returned her attention to Hoops. She smiled. "Are you going to reveal to me my fortune and that of my realm? I understand Wiffins possess extraordinary talents of all sorts. Thus, I'd not be surprised to hear you're clairvoyant."

"I'm but a simple fisherman and hunter. I have no great gifts of mind or magic," said Hoops, bowing his head humbly.

"Then you're not going to read me my fortune?"

"Absolutely not, My Lady. I believe your future and that of Sar rests entirely in your capable hands. Am I not correct in saying that your forebears, and you, all struggled against great odds to create this magnificent kingdom? The responsibility—the duty—to preserve, even strengthen, the realm now rests solely on Your Majesty's shoulders."

The queen nodded. "That's why I don't sleep so well at night, Wiffin."

"Because you worry about the enemies lurking within the kingdom? Because you can envision violence and anarchy exploding throughout the land if it were not for Your Majesty—the warrior queen—uniting the realm against the archenemy, the Lughs?"

Saragata nodded and briefly closed her eyes as if trying to relive one of her nightmares. The room grew even chillier, as the fire on the hearth burnt down to glowing embers.

Hoops boldly interrupted her thoughts. "The cement that holds this fragile kingdom together is you, Your Majesty, because only a united Sar stands as an impregnable wall between your subjects and their enslavement by the Lughs!"

The queen glanced down once again at the gold box nestled in the palm of her pale but strong hand. "Shortly, there will be no need for that wall of protection, Wiffin. You and I both know the power of this talisman. It means the total destruction of the Lughs. There will be everlasting peace for my kingdom."

"That's the whole point!" Hoops realized he was shouting. That wasn't the way to talk to a queen. He immediately lowered his voice. "I do not wish to be so bold as to state the obvious to Your Highness. Naturally, you realize that, once the external threat of a Lugh invasion is forever eliminated, your internal foes will no longer see the need for a united Sar under your rule. Surely, ancient rivalries and animosities will soon rekindle, splintering apart your kingdom. Your worst fears will be realized. Internal strife and bloodshed—not internal peace and prosperity—will rule the countryside. You may wake one morning to find the Goddess of Chaos seated in triumph upon your throne."

The queen again shut her eyes, her mouth pinched, her face pale. She pulled her gown closer about her to ward off a chill. *A chill from without or from within?* Hoops wondered. He patiently waited for her to break the silence. Holding her handkerchief to her mouth, Saragata suffered a bout of deep, throaty coughs. Once they subsided, the queen opened her eyes and stared hard at Hoops. "So, what would you have me do, Wiffin?"

"Simply do not use the talisman," Hoops answered bluntly. "Continue the never-ending conflict with the Lughs. The wars have kept your kingdom alive and strong over the past generations. They will continue to do so, unless, of course, you allow that talisman to spring into action."

"I'm beginning to understand why you, your astute grandfather, and even Tajine did not wish to see the talisman fall into my possession." She paused to cough several times. "I wonder what our God of War, Brutius, would think," she said. "He has always been so insistent that I secure the talisman and wipe out the Lughs. I wonder if he's considered the consequences if I did so. Would the people of this kingdom tolerate lavish spending on the feasts, temples, and shrines he so craves once his help is no longer needed in a conflict with an archenemy? I doubt it."

"Frankly, I do, too," said Hoops.

She smiled ironically. Then, a look of sadness veiled her liquid eyes. "I have serious doubts that I can do what you suggest, Wiffin. I may be forced to risk everything and employ the talisman against the Lughs."

"That's silly. You're the queen. You can do as you please!" Hoops took a deep breath. *Wrong thing to say to a queen,* he thought. You don't tell a powerful monarch she's silly.

"What I meant to say, your most kind Majesty, is that I don't understand why you believe you may have to use the talisman when

you clearly recognize it's not in your kingdom's best interest to do so."
He hoped that sounded more diplomatic.

"Unless I'm mistaken, no one in this realm but you, I, your cat-witch Zaggie, Itus, and presumably that Gretien girl know the significance of what I'm holding in my hand." She held the box closer to the firelight, studying the carefree, playful crimson reflections dancing on its gilded surface.

"Javala is aware only that the talisman could play a role in the fate of Sar. Nothing more, Your Majesty. As for the new witch of Dourghoul—"

"My concern is not the girl, nor Zaggie, nor you," the queen interrupted. "It is Itus. My lord general has an all-consuming desire to bring about the complete destruction of the Kingdom of the Lughs. It's that passion that has made him such a great military leader. I fear he's capable of doing anything, even plotting against his own queen, if necessary, to see his dream realized. He's not necessarily loved by his soldiers, but as a leader, he's justifiably earned the respect of many legionnaires. I regret to admit it, but he has established a powerful following within the military. Do you understand what I'm saying, Wiffin?"

"Could you not explain to him what the annihilation of the Lughs would mean for him? He'd be a general without a great enemy to fight. There would no longer be medals of valor to be earned, nor triumphal parades, or—"

Again, the queen stopped him mid-sentence. "Unlike Brutius, Itus doesn't care about medals or parades. All that matters to the lord general is victory on a corpse-strewn battlefield. If, as you suggest, uprisings and civil wars will follow the final defeat of the Lughs, Itus will still find happiness by slaughtering rebellious subjects. No, little Wiffin! Itus will not be swayed by that argument."

"Then give me the talisman and let me take it away to my neutral homeland for safekeeping."

The queen smiled, but it lacked warmth. "That idea crossed my mind while we've been speaking. But, alas, I dare not underestimate what a furious Itus might do when he's realized what has happened. As you must realize by now, the general is ruthless when angered.

I can ill afford risking an Itus-led rebellion within the ranks of my military." A deep sigh escaped her lips. "In any case, Wiffin, I cannot let you leave here unpunished. As I told you when we first met, my subjects expect me to handle your case as if you were a Sarien subject found guilty of treasonable activities. Once again, I imagine my entire realm is humming with news of your latest betrayal. I am, indeed, sorry about this whole incident. But this time, you've left me no other option."

"What if Itus should die?" Hoops blurted out, fully aware that what had crossed his mind was utterly ridiculous, totally hopeless.

"What do you mean, Wiffin?" Saragata's voice was icy, suspicious. "You'd best explain yourself this very instant!"

"I realize that I'm facing death. So be it. But you must admit, Your Majesty, that I intended to do both you and your kingdom a favor. Although ill-fated, my intentions were honorable."

Saragata nodded. "It seems that way, Wiffin. So you expect a favor in return?"

"Yes," replied Hoops. "All I ask is that I be entitled to choose the manner in which I die. I know you can make suitable arrangements, Your Majesty, if you so wish."

"Of course, I can, Wiffin. But I deeply regret having to make any such arrangements at all," she said grimly. "How do you wish to die? I'll make whatever arrangements you request."

"Then please schedule a duel between Itus and myself," Hoops replied in a shaken voice. "Naturally, it will be a duel to the death."

Chapter 20

A pallid dawn spread slender fingers of diffused gray light over a city entrapped beneath a thick layer of wet snow. Hoops stood by the single window of a sparsely furnished, unheated chamber adjacent to the queen's private offices. He clutched his green cloak tightly about his shoulders to ward off the chill but he couldn't help shivering. Below the window close to the palace walls stood the oblong arena, enclosed by tiers of stone benches. Workmen in ragged fur jackets were busy with straw brooms, sweeping the seats clear of snow. A canopy of blue and gold silk had been erected at one end of the arena, presumably for the queen and the royal entourage. He heard a series of low coughs. He turned to find the queen standing in the doorway. A faint smile played across her lips, but her eyes reflected sadness.

"I hope I didn't startle you," she said, as she silently walked over to Hoops's side and gazed down at the scene below. "I wish they wouldn't insist on such a bright, gaudy canopy on such occasions as these. I think something subdued would be more appropriate. But we must do our royal best to entertain the spectators, mustn't we?"

Hoops nodded.

"Are you certain you won't reconsider, little Wiffin? I know Itus all too well. I have ridden at his side into many battles. He will not kill you outright, although he easily could. No, Wiffin, he'll take great pleasure in toying with you, making you suffer as long as possible before he decides to strike the final blow. Besides, he wants to please the mob of spectators. The more blood you spill turning that

144

snow crimson the louder will be cheers from the mob. Itus adores cheering crowds."

"I have made up my mind, Your Majesty. I'll fight Itus." Saragata sighed. "As I told you last night, Wiffin, my chief executor swears that beheading is the fastest and least painful way to an afterlife. I promised you that will be Javala's fate once you're dead. It would be so much easier for you if you choose the same fate."

"But if I win this duel? You promised last night that, in that unlikely event, you would allow me to take the girl with me to my country."

"I did agree to that, little Wiffin, and I stand behind my word. But don't forget that you, in turn, agreed that she would remain in exile in your country unless I feel my relations with the Gretien are such than I can risk having that little troublemaker return home."

The queen turned away from the window to face Hoops. "After our conversation last night, I went down to the dungeons to advise Javala of our agreement. As expected, she was abusive and, at first, insisted on dying a martyr, no matter the outcome of your duel with Itus. It took a while, but I finally convinced her that would do nothing to help her clansmen. Of course, she will be beheaded. We all have to face reality. Itus will kill you in this duel. I regret, however, that the girl will go to her death believing I was responsible for the slaughter of most of her family and so many of her countrymen. I swear, Hoops, I never anticipated that massacre would take place. But as queen, I guess I must take ultimate responsibility for that tragedy. Just more guilt to burden my wretched soul."

The queen reached behind her neck and unfastened a thin chain bearing a small oval piece of raw gold. "Put out your hand, Wiffin." She dropped the necklace into his open palm. "It is an ancient charm against evil," she explained. "My royal father gave it to me when I was a child. Wear it under your tunic when you face Itus this morning. I do not for a moment believe it will help spare your life, but perhaps it will make your death less agonizing." She reached between the folds of her long black gown and retrieved another item of gold. It was one of Javala's earrings. "The Gretien removed this from her ear and gave it to me to present to you as a parting gift." She turned back to the window. "I see the spectators forming outside the arena gates. And the trumpeters already are assembled. I'm afraid I must leave you now. The queen must ready herself to greet her loyal subjects and announce the beginning of the duel." She turned to go, stopped, and looked back at Hoops. "Captain Gartho and his weary band of Fourth Legionnaires finally arrived here shortly after the bewitching hour this morning. He asked to have a final word with you before you entered the arena, assuming you agree?"

Hoops nodded. "Farewell, Your Majesty. I wish only the very best for you and your realm."

The queen smiled and slipped out of the room. A moment later, Captain Gartho tramped through the door. He looked tired and gaunt. His hardened features were stretched taut.

"You are a total fool, Hoops!" he growled. "You can't possibly defeat the great lord general. He's going to torture you first. He'll use a spiked mace to break your knees first, then your elbows. Then he'll mash open your stomach till your guts are scattered all over the snow. But you'll still be alive and pleading for death. Maybe then, and only then, he might take pity and crush your skull. Do you understand what I'm telling you, Wiffin? Tell the queen now that you've changed your mind and will join the Gretien girl at the chopping block. Please, Hoops! Use your brains while you still have some left in your head!"

Hoops shook his head. "I appreciate your concern, Gartho. Believe me, I do, but I must risk this battle with the general. Besides the life of the girl, there is more at stake here than you know. Don't ask me to explain."

"I find all this hard to believe, Wiffin. The queen even tells me you refuse to use a sword or wear any armor. You insist on fighting Itus with just your little belt ax. Simply incredible!" the captain exploded. He reached for the sword at his belt. "I insist that you use my weapon, Wiffin!"

Hoops raised his hand in protest. "Thank you for your offer, Captain, but I don't know how to handle a sword properly. I've never worn armor. That would only slow me down. Agility is all I have going for me today, Gartho. And my little ax."

With a deep sigh of frustration, the captain turned away from Hoops and looked out the window. "The arena is filling up. I see Itus himself has entered. He's in full armor, carrying a shield. As I predicted, he's got his spiked mace in hand. I cannot make out his facial expressions from here, but I wager he's grinning at the very thought of splattering your blood over the entire arena."

"Doubtless, you're right, Gartho," Hoops said. "I want to thank you, Captain, for trying to talk me out of this. I sincerely appreciate your efforts, even though they were in vain."

Gartho suddenly lowered his voice to a half whisper. "One final piece of advice, Wiffin. Itus does not see well out of his right eye. He's lost his right ear and his right hand in battles because of this. If you hope to have any chance at all against him, stay to his right and strike from that side." Having said that, the stone-faced Gartho stomped out of the room.

Almost immediately, a youthful-looking palace guard appeared in the doorway. "It is almost time for the spectacle to begin, Wiffin." The guard handed Hoops a sheathed hunting knife. "The queen said she believes it belongs to you, and you might find some use for it today." Hoops tucked his knife in his belt. Now he had both an ax and a hunting knife with which to face Itus. He hadn't forgotten the skinning knife still concealed in his boot, but what use would that little blade be against a giant in full armor?

"It's time to go, Wiffin," said the guard. "Please follow me."

Chapter 21

Despite the harsh cold and the threat of more snow, an overflowing crowd jostled for seats or standing room. Cheers mixed with outbursts of raucous laughter greeted Hoops accompanied by the palace guard, as they stepped into view.

"He's not much bigger than my three-year-old grandson!" yelled someone in the crowd. Another explosion of laughter.

"No wonder he ain't wearing no armor," shouted another spectator. "They couldn't find nothing in the armory small enough to fit 'em!" More guffaws.

The blare of trumpets momentarily drowned out the roar of the crowd as the queen entered the arena and proceeded to a throne beneath the canopy. Courtiers, ministers, aides, military officers, and assorted advisors streamed into the arena in her wake. Javala arrived last. Two soldiers escorted the girl to a tall wooden pole sunk into the earth near the royal canopy. Her hands were unbound, but a bronze chain attached to a collar about her neck secured her to the post. The soldiers flanked her. One of them, Hoops noticed, was an archer. The second soldier struggled with a confused and agitated Havoc on a thin leather leash. Another blast of trumpets. Through the main arena gates marched a contingent of colorful clowns, jugglers, dancing bears with their trainers, and prancing horses with riders adorned with fake armor.

"What is all this?" Hoops asked of the palace guard.

"It's a bit of a circus. Whenever there's an official duel, it's a cause for celebration among the city folk. This one is a shade more elaborate than usual because the royal production managers don't believe the duel between you and the lord general will last very long. Hence, they hope to compensate by presenting the crowd with a spectacular preamble."

The temperature was dropping dramatically. The prancing horses, bears, and jugglers trampled the wet snow covering the dirt floor of the arena. Hoops noticed the slush was turning rapidly to ice. Several times, clowns lost their footing. A bear slipped and slammed headlong against the arena's lowest tier of seats, sending terrified onlookers scrambling for safety. Hoops ignored the rest of the show. He focused on Itus who was engaged in an animated conversation with several legionnaires on the far side of the arena.

Itus had his large bronze shield in his iron claw. In his left hand, he effortlessly dangled a mace—a heavy iron ball embedded with sharp bronze spikes attached to a long wooden handle. Hoops doubted he was capable of picking up Itus's weapon even if he used both hands. The general cradled a full helmet including a nose guard in the crook of his elbow. A leather cuirass adorned with a battered bronze breastplate covered his chest. He wore gauntlets. Bronze protected his shins. A black tunic reached almost to his knees.

Hoops suffered a spasm of despair. Except for his exposed thighs, upper arms, and neck, Itus appeared invulnerable, even if Hoops was able to bypass the general's shield. Hoops looked back at Javala. The girl impassively gazed straight ahead. Except to brush strands of breeze-taunted red hair from her eyes, she remained motionless. Behind her sat the queen bundled in a black fur cape.

Saragata glanced briefly at Hoops, her features entirely devoid of expression. She raised her hand. The trumpets sounded. The performers scrambled to empty the arena, dragging with them the assortment of circus animals. Sleet began pelting the City of Sar. The crowd falls silent.

"Let the duel begin," the queen announced in a clear, emotionless voice.

On the other side of the arena, the lord general fitted his bronze shield to his right forearm and donned his helmet. Mace in his left hand, he strolled to the center of the arena to await Hoops. Hoops couldn't move. His feet seemed bound in blocks of ice. He heard the young palace guard beside him say, "You can't tum back now, Wiffin. Go face the general! But first, remove your cloak. You can't fight with that hanging over your shoulders." Hoops shrugged off the green wool robe and handed it to the guard. "Please have it. It once belonged to a great sorceress." The youth looked hesitant.

"Don't worry," Hoops said. "It won't turn you into a frog. Please take it. I fear I will never again have use for a cloak." Hoops took a deep breath and, ax in trembling right hand, walked slowly through the ice-encrusted sludge toward Itus.

The general struck first. With a low, sweeping swing, Itus aimed his mace at Hoops's right knee. Hoops jumped backward, trying to get out of range. But he wasn't fast enough. He felt a sharp pain in his thigh. He glanced down to see flecks of blood splatter the snow at his feet. But he was still on his feet. One of the mace's sharp iron points had just grazed his flesh. At the sight of first blood, a roar went up from the onlookers. "I promise you, the next blow will crush that already gimpy right knee, Wiffin." Itus laughed sardonically. "Then I'll smash your left knee. And that will be just the beginning."

Hoops stepped backward, trying to stay just out of range of the mace. "Why do you hate me so, General? After all, I saved your life in the Great Mire."

"That's exactly why I despise you, little Wiffin. You did save my life. Twice, in fact. So I'm indebted to you. I'm also indebted to that wretched Gretien girl for saving my beloved horse." He feigned another blow at Hoops's legs and laughed as Hoops scrambled and almost fell in a desperate effort to get out of range. "I rose through the ranks because of my own strength and my own wits, Wiffin. I received no help from anyone along the way. I hate you and the girl because, for once, I'm obligated to you. But with your deaths, so end my debts." He twirled the heavy mace in his hand like it was a featherweight walking stick.

"But you owe the queen, Itus. She appointed you commander of her army."

"I'll let you in on a little secret, Hoops. My talents alone earned me the title. She may think I'm indebted to her, but it won't be long before I'll rid myself of her. Sar will have a new ruler. Namely, myself."

Suddenly, Itus lashed out again with a sweeping stroke of the mace aimed at Hoops's knee. This time, Hoops sprung back in time. The weapon missed his limb by a fraction of an inch.

The crowd roared, "Blood! We want blood!" Itus took his eyes off Hoops and glanced around at the onlookers. He raised both his mace and his shield high in the air to acknowledge their shouts.

"Now!" Hoops muttered aloud, as he shifted his ax from his right to his left hand. With a sidearm motion, he threw the weapon, aiming at the general's momentarily exposed right thigh.

The instant Hoops released the ax, he knew he was too late. Itus, eyes still focused on the crowd and unaware of the ax hurtling through the icy air toward his blind side, lowered the shield just in time. A metallic clang resounded as the ax slammed against the bottom edge of the shield and ricocheted into the air, landing several paces away in the snow well out of Hoops's reach. Another roar of excitement went up from the spectators. Itus seemed briefly stunned by what happened. "Luck was almost with you, Wiffin. But I'll not let that happen again, believe me!"

Hoops desperately pulled his hunting knife from his belt. Holding it low, well out in front of his body, he began circling Itus, seeking an opportunity to rush in close enough for an upward thrust with the blade. Itus violently swung his mace again. This time, the general aimed for Hoops's upper body. Hoops dropped instantly to a crouch, but instinctively, he raised his hand holding the knife to ward off a blow. The spiked iron ball swished over his head, but the wooden mace shaft jarred against his forearm. He heard the sharp snap of a bone breaking. The knife spun out of his grasp, sailing through the sleet-filled air. It landed in the white arena sludge far from the combatants.

The crowd cheered. Itus laughed. "One bone broken, Wiffin, but we still have many more to attend to." The giant swung again—another low aim—directed at Hoops's legs. Hoops jumped backward to get out of range, but his right foot slipped on the ice and he fell to the ground. He found himself on his back, looking up at Itus towering over him, mace raised for another blow. "Now, the fun begins," muttered the giant, white teeth gleaming in a diabolical smile.

Hoops heard someone yell hoarsely, "The wolf's loose!" Itus glanced in the direction of the shout. His mace remained hovered in the air. Out of the comer of his eye, Hoops saw a blur of reddish brown fur streaking straight for Itus from the general's right. Itus was slow to react. Havoc sank his fangs into the exposed flesh just above the general's right knee. Itus, wincing in pain, staggered backward but regained his footing and struck hard. Blood and brains exploded into the air as the mace crushed Havoc's skull. Hoops howled in rage. Drawing his skinning knife from his boot with his left hand, he struggled to his feet and charged the general's right side. Itus spun to meet Hoops. But his movement was too abrupt, the ground too icy. The general lost his footing and slipped on the ice. He went down on one knee. The jolt sent his helmet slithering across the freezing ground. His mace falls from his hand.

As Itus struggled to regain his feet, Hoops flung himself upon the general, the knife pointed at the giant's throat. The blade plunged the hilt into the general's massive, sinewed neck just beneath the jaw. A purplish, pulsating stream of blood spewed from Itus's severed jugular. Hoops's face, sprayed by blood gushing from the mortal wound, was barely two inches from. Itus's. Their eyes met briefly. Hoops saw only disbelief reflected in the dying man's expression. A gurgling sound rumbled from the general's throat. Itus went limp. He collapsed backward against the crimson-smeared ice and lay still. Hoops slowly got to his feet, his broken right arm dangling uselessly at his side. He glanced at Havoc's body surrounded by a spreading pool of blood. "Please, Zob, treat him kindly in the afterlife. He died bravely."

Hoops fought back a wave of nausea. He wasn't sure where the sickening feeling arouse, from the sight of his slaughtered wolf or from the stark realization that for the first time in his life he had taken the life of another human being. He turned his back on the carnage and, with blurred eyes and on unsteady feet, slowly made his way across the arena toward the queen's throne.

A hush descended over the arena. "Watch out behind you, Hoops!"

Hoops looked up in time to see Javala ram her elbow into the groin of the archer beside her. As the soldier doubled over in pain, Javala grabbed his bow, whipped an arrow from his quiver, fit it to the bowstring, drew, and let fly. Hoops heard a sickening thud behind him. He spun around to see Itus, bathed in crimson and swaying but on his feet once more, only a few paces away. In the general's left hand poised the mace, readied to strike. But with his iron claw, Itus clutched desperately at the shaft of the arrow Javala had buried deep in his right eye. Hoops thought he heard a final utterance—"Damned Gretien wretch!"—before the lord general staggered forward, faltered, and fell face down into a pool of his own blood. One of his legs twitched several times, then stilled.

Two legionnaires raced across the snow to where he lay. "The lord general is dead," one announced in a loud voice to the queen.

The crowd went into an uproar, chanting, "Wiffin! Wiffin! Wiffin!" over and over again.

Hoops approached Saragata's throne. He glanced at Javala. She was beaming. She handed the bow back to her guard who was still clutching his stomach, groaning in pain.

"Approach the throne, Wiffin," ordered a stern-faced Saragata. Hoops obeyed. "It is customary for the queen to present a trophy to the victor in an official duel," she announced for all to hear. She held up a little gold casket for the crowd to see, then she handed it to Hoops. She lowered her voice to almost a whisper. "I've given this a great deal of thought, and I've concluded that you and your grandfather should be custodians of this dreadful talisman. I trust you will keep it in a safe place when you return home, Hoops."

"I assure you, we will do so, Your Majesty."

The queen turned to one of her aides and told him to alert the palace physician that she was sending Hoops to him shortly. "Inform the Grand Healer I want this Wiffin's injuries attended to immediately. He and the Gretien girl have a lengthy voyage ahead. I want him to arrive home in good health." The aide bowed and sprinted off toward the palace. "Where's my admiral of the fleet?" the queen barked.

A bearded gentleman with a black eye patch emerged from the entourage surrounding the throne and bowed to her majesty.

"When is our next scheduled sea battle with the Lughs, Admiral?"

"Because of the current inclement weather, we have all agreed to postpone until two months hence," was the reply.

"Excellent! That should free up a few long ships. You are to escort the Wiffin's vessel as far as Horn Harbor. I wish to be certain the Wiffin and his Gretien passenger do not run afoul of Lugh raiders or pirates on their way home."

Hoops said in a low voice, "Beg your pardon, Your Majesty, but that is not necessary. I'm sure my vessel can outrun any Lugh or pirate ships on the high seas."

The queen answered in an equally low voice. "I beg your pardon, little Wiffin. Perhaps you're right, but I'm not taking any chances!"

Saragata gazed out over the assembled entourage. "Where is the general?"

"General Itus is dead, Your Highness!" exclaimed Scotus in his shrill voice.

Saragata burst into a fit of rage. She gripped the arms of her throne so tightly her knuckles turned white. She glared at Scotus and shouted, "Of course, I know Itus is dead, you sad excuse for a human being. I've tolerated your giggling, your whining, your whimpering, and your stupid advice. I'll not have you insult my intelligence! You are hereby dismissed as my inquisitor, you wimp! In fact, you're hereby banished from this city!" She turned to her palace guards. "Get this miserable creature out of my sight!"

The entire assembly held its breath, waiting for the queen to calm down. Saragata's hands gradually relaxed their grip on the arms of the chair and color returned to her knuckles. The crowd breathed a collective sigh of relief. "Now, would General Gartho be so kind as to step forward," Saragata said gently.

Gartho, who was standing among a group of his legionnaires at the edge of the arena, glanced around him, his normally rock-hard eyes betraying bewilderment. A legionnaire nudged him forward. Gartho, hunched over and looking totally confused, stumbled across the ice and approached the queen.

Saragata leaned forward and said in a whisper that only Hoops, standing beside the throne, could hear, "General Gartho, please stand up straight and try to look like the commander of my army."

Gartho snapped to attention and saluted.

"Much better, General," remarked the queen. She followed this comment with a string of crisp orders: secure supplies including foodstuffs and water from the palace storehouse for Hoops's voyage home; make certain Hoops and Javala were properly clothed for the journey; make suitable arrangements for shipping Havoc's remains to Horn Harbor; and finally, have an escort of Fourth Legionnaires led by the new general himself to accompany Hoops and Javala to wherever Hoops's boat was hidden and see them off safely.

Gartho assured Saragata all her commands would be carried out promptly. He saluted her, turned to Hoops and saluted him and marched off to gather his troops for the mission.

Hoops reached inside his jerkin and felt the little nugget of gold the queen had given him before the duel. "I must return your necklace, Your Majesty. It served me well."

"Please keep it, Wiffin, as a small token of my appreciation for all you've done here. Perhaps, someday, it will again serve you well." The queen looked over at Javala. The Gretien stood silently, eyes fixed on the ground, seemingly unaware of the bustling activity around her. "Exile will be hard on the girl, Hoops. Please, promise me that you and your wise grandfather will do everything you can to make her life in Horn Harbor as pleasant as possible."

"I promise we will, Your Majesty."

Chapter 22

"Where are we now?" asked Armarugh, gazing out at the sea. He and Hoops were seated in the stern of the little fishing boat. The sky was clear blue. A crisp breeze filled the mainsail.

"We're sailing over Wolftrap Canyon. We're about four nautical miles outside the mouth of the harbor."

"How deep is the water here, Hoops?"

"Very deep. I'd say roughly seventy-five fathoms. Why do you ask, Grandfather?"

Armarugh didn't answer. Instead, he reached inside his heavy black cloak, withdrew the gold talisman casket, and tossed it into the sea. Hoops let go of the tiller, leapt to his feet, and rushed to the gunwale. The gold box had already sunk from view in the murky, frigid water.

"Do you know what you've just done, Armarugh? Nobody will ever be able to recover it!"

"I certainly hope not, my dear grandson. I do not want to risk having that cursed talisman ever fall into the wrong hands. There are people in this world, Hoops, who might use it recklessly, regardless of the consequences. Believe me, there are many such fools roaming this world."

The vessel momentarily veered off course, and the sail luffed. Hoops grabbed the tiller to coax the craft back on a steady course.

Perplexed, Hoops said, "You said that everyone who is aware of the talisman's existence knows we have it and that we will use it against anyone who threatens us. Now, thanks to you, Grandfather, it no longer exists, except at the bottom of the sea. We couldn't use it if we had to. I can't believe what you've just done! We are defenseless!"

"The talisman does exist, Hoops. It exists in the minds, in the imaginations of those who fear it most. It may be at the bottom of the sea, but it will always serve our purpose—even that of Queen Saragata—as long as its legend continues to exist," Armarugh said emphatically. "Trust me, Hoops, I plan to take measures to perpetuate that legend for all eternity."

"I still don't understand, Grandfather. Why didn't you just put the talisman away somewhere for safekeeping? Hide it in your cavern, for example?" asked Hoops, as he eased out the mainsheet to compensate for an unexpected increase in the easterly wind.

"Don't be naive, my dear Hoops. There are too many Wiffins who are aware the talisman has come to rest in our quiet land. All the members of the council, for example. We, Wiffins, like to pride ourselves on good sense, moderation, control of our passions, honesty, and so forth and so on. Nevertheless, Hoops, there are those among us who, despite outward appearances, have a lust for power lurking just beneath the surface. You will not live forever. Nor will I. The angel of death, as Zaggie always calls her, may tap me on the shoulder any day. The tap could come in the form of a bad cold or from a morsel of your improperly salted fish. Who knows? In any event, when I'm dead, I want to be certain no power-craving idiot starts rummaging through my effects and finds the talisman."

"But when the elders and others find out what you've done—"

"Hoops, please, calm yourself. You and I are the only ones who know what transpired today. We intend to keep it that way, don't we, dear grandson?"

"Of course, Grandfather," Hoops said, although he still felt anxiety over what Armarugh had just done.

The old magus glanced up at the sky. "It may be a sunny day, Hoops, but it's winter and I feel chilly. Also, I wish this boat wouldn't keel over so far on its side. It makes me uneasy."

"A sailboat heels. It doesn't keel, Grandfather," replied Hoops with a grin. "Since it appears we've accomplished our mission, I suggest I bring her about and we head for home."

"Splendid idea!" The sorcerer retrieved a small green flask from under the folds of his cloak, uncorked it, and took a sip.

"What's that?" Hoops inquired.

"Oh, just a little something medicinal. Helps ward off seasickness and the like."

Neither exchanged words for a few minutes. The wind hummed in the shrouds and water murmured against the hull as the craft knifed through the sea toward the narrow harbor entrance. "You never did explain who was the hunter I met back in Sar. I told you he sent his regards," Hoops commented.

Armarugh frowned. "I'm not sure myself, Hoops. Perhaps he was only a figment of your imagination. Or of mine." Hoops recognized from his grandfather's tone that the topic of the hunter was dismissed. Armarugh changed the subject. "I must say that the elders are impressed with your leadership of a rejuvenated Defense Council. Your idea of having that Gretien girl teach archery to our young Wiffins was quite brilliant. I realize there was a lot of protesting at the start. Our young men were not at all happy with her muscle building and calisthenics programs."

"I'm sure they weren't, Armarugh, but Javala was disgusted that so few of our would-be soldiers had enough strength to bend the string to the bow, let alone draw it. But from what I've observed, they're gradually getting rather proficient with those weapons she designed for them. Now that my arm's healed, I plan to take lessons from her as well. I've always considered myself somewhat of a good bowman, but when I watch her split a pear in half at a hundred paces, I know I still have a lot to learn from that girl."

The Wise One nodded. "Speaking of Javala, I realize she's not entirely happy being in exile here and wants to return to her clansmen. I've word from Queen Saragata that she has made great headway in negotiating a peace agreement with Javala's brother. Perhaps Javala will be allowed to return home sooner than we all expected. Which reminds me, I forgot to tell you that hardworking Zaggie has discovered a magical cure for that disease that almost decimated the Gretien livestock this past year."

"Has Zaggie developed her telepathic abilities to the extent she can communicate with you all the way from Dourghoul Keep?" Hoops asked the wizard.

"Not yet, but she's making progress. In the meantime, that furry little Yukman is letting her borrow his personal falcon to ferry messages back and forth. Zaggie also expects to master the skill of flying fairly soon and should be paying us a visit shortly."

Again, the two fell silent as the vessel sliced through the channel separating Horn Harbor from the sea. The water became calmer, although the breeze remained steady.

"What do you think of Javala's artwork so far, Grandfather?"

"The truth?"

"Of course." The wizard paused to compose his thoughts before replying. "I know she can draw with uncanny accuracy, but I don't understand her paintings. For instance, in my thinking, a painting of a tree should look like a tree. But when Javala paints a tree, I'm a shade perplexed. The painting will be very pleasing, very colorful, and I'd say, extremely dramatic. In fact, I'd call it dynamic. But I'm not always convinced I'm staring at a real tree."

Hoops nodded. "I must admit, her style is different."

"To say the least, Hoops. Her instructors, great masters all, rave about her paintings. Betadini, for example, says he considers Javala the most talented student he's ever tutored. He calls her a *gifted revolutionary in the world of art*. I must confess, Hoops, art is one of the few subjects I've never really understood, so I have to bow to Betadini's judgment."

Hoops laughed. "I'm pleased to hear you finally admit, Wise One, that there's at least one subject in which you're not an expert."

Armarugh humbly bowed his head, glanced at Hoops and said earnestly, "Please don't repeat my remarks about her paintings to Javala. She might take offense. Believe it or not, she can make even your hardened, jaded grandfather feel a wee bit uncomfortable when her beautiful, soft green eyes turn to icy, hard emeralds whenever I foolishly mention Saragata or the Sariens in front of her."

Hoops grinned. "A lot of folks feel the same, Grandfather, including myself. I just thank Zob she tolerates me." They were rounding a spit of marsh, rapidly approaching their destination. "I hope the elders have finally abandoned their silly notion of insisting Javala paint a mural of my duel with Itus for the council building. It would be an embarrassment for me. In any case, I'd prefer never to be reminded that event took place," Hoops said vehemently.

"Don't worry. Javala refused to paint one and for much the same reasons. She blames herself for all that happened to you. She's confided to me she never before felt so guilty, so helpless, and so much in despair as when she watched you walk into that arena to face Itus. But on a lighter note, Hoops, I'm staging a dinner in my humble abode for Haro, the great sculptor who designed the magnificent monument dedicated to our faithful, stout-hearted Havoc. Haro now is insisting that Javala becomes one of his students. Naturally, I've invited Javala over to meet him, and I would appreciate you joining us. I'm personally preparing the meal. Trust me, Hoops, it will prove absolutely delicious."

Hoops glanced away so the wizard would not see him grimace. Armarugh was renowned for being the worst chef in all Horn Harbor. Hoops's past experiences at the wizard's dinner table convinced him the sorcerer's title was well deserved. "Of course, I accept your kind invitation, Grandfather," Hoops replied, hoping his tone of voice didn't betray his reluctance.

They came within sight of the cove not far from the dank cavern the wizard called home. Javala stood on the shoreline, as usual, to welcome Hoops back from a voyage. She was gleefully waving both arms in the air. Not unexpectedly, a bow and a quiver hung over her shoulder. "As much as I like and admire that girl, I wish she would agree to wear the robes and gowns we've presented her," muttered Armarugh. "But she persists on dressing like she's about to leap astride a war horse and charge into battle." Javala, laughing, eyes sparkling, dashed out into the cold water to help them drag the vessel up on the narrow beach.

Hoops whispered to his grandfather, "I'm concerned that if Saragata dies prematurely, whoever accedes to the throne might elect to make more trouble for the Gretiens. If that happens, I can easily envision Javala astride a war horse, bow in hand, riding full fury into the midst of battle."

"Aye, Hoops," Armarugh whispered back. "In that event, I wouldn't be surprised to see my own grandson, ax in hand, shaking in his boots, riding into the fray at her side. But first, Javala is going to have to teach you to ride," said the wizard with a wry chuckle. "And secondly, Hoops, I suggest you get a bigger ax."

About the Author

As a former journalist and retired intelligence officer, Jackson Galbraith has weaved into this action-oriented, fast-paced fantasy just enough parallelism with real world national and international politics to help stimulate the thinking of youthful readers along these lines.

Jack has lived in several foreign countries, worked with newspapers, was an editor with UPI, and eventually entered the foreign service. After retiring, he worked on novels and became a professional artist.

Gloucester Library
P.O. Box 2380
Gloucester, VA 23061

CPSIA information can be obtained
at www.ICGtesting.com
Printed in the USA
BVHW07s1522090718
521160BV00005B/362/P